A MESSAGE

It's hot in our yard. I'm happy to open the door to the house, which is built of concrete blocks and is always shady and cool. I see a piece of paper stuck under the door, just inside. I pick it up.

"Mama! Paloma! I'm home." She always wants to know, even if she's taking a shower out back in the washhouse.

Paloma doesn't answer. And Romy's not around, either. Maybe they're out together. I read the note while I'm going for a glass of water. The handwriting is clumsy. Bigger and shakier than Romy's.

LEAVE AND DON'T COME BACK. IF NOT, <u>YOU</u> DIE.

Critical acclaim for *Grab Hands and Run*

School Library Journal Best Books of the Year

Booklist Editors' Choice

Bank Street College of Education Children's
Book of the Year Selection

"The characters come vividly to life, in their courageous behavior and in Temple's telling language; the grueling journey typifies the Latino refugee experience. . . . Well wrought, authentic, and compelling." (pointer review)

— *The Kirkus Reviews*

"Although the book does not delve into the details of Salvadoran politics . . . the danger is made shockingly clear. Temple's narrative as seen through Felipe's eyes conveys differences of language, culture, and landscape in a subtle but tangible way, and through brief episodes she paints a strong and suspenseful picture of their life before and during their journey, as well as in a United States detention center." (starred review)

—*School Library Journal*

"Vivid . . . poignant. . . . A good read for its own sake as well as a chilling account of totalitarianism and displaced persons." (starred review)

—ALA *Booklist*

"Details of the brutal realities in El Salvador are dexterously woven into the story of one family's struggle to beat the odds. . . . A sustained level of suspense spurs readers on." (starred review)

—*Publishers Weekly*

Grab Hands and Run

Frances Temple

HarperTrophy®
A Division of HarperCollinsPublishers

ALSO BY FRANCES TEMPLE

Taste of Salt
A STORY OF MODERN HAITI

Harper Trophy® is a registered trademark of HarperCollins Publishers Inc.

Grab Hands and Run
Copyright © 1993 by Frances Nolting Temple
For information address HarperCollins Children's Books, a division of HarperCollins Publishers, 10 East 53rd street, New York, NY 10022.
Reprinted by arrangement with Orchard Books, New York.
Book Design by Mina Greenstein
LC Number 92-34063
Trophy ISBN 0-06-440548-6
First Harper Trophy edition, 1995.

Thanks to Manlio Argueta for the inspiration of his novels, *One Day of Life* and *Cuzcatlán*, published in Spanish by UCA Editores, San Salvador, and in English by Aventura/Random House, New York, in 1983 and 1987, respectively.

Thanks to Ariel Dorfman for realizations springing from his collection of poems, *Last Waltz in Santiago*, Penguin/Viking, New York, 1988.

Thanks to Renny Golden and Michael McConnell for information in their book *Sanctuary* (Orbis, Maryknoll, New York, 1986), to Amnesty International and Americas Watch for recording the words and thoughts of people in flight, and to all those brave enough to testify.

Thanks to people at *Proyecto Canada* and in the Geneva, New York, interfaith community.

Thanks most of all to I.M., for companionship, stories, and good times.

—F.T.

To V.C.M., to H.C.M., and to Tyler

Grab Hands and Run

1

The Lagoon

"FELIPE!"

"*Sí, Abuela. . . .*"

"Felipe, *patito*, don't float out so far!"

Little duck, she calls me. I'm twelve years old, not so very little. I am not tall, but I have big feet. Which, according to my father Jacinto, indicate that I will grow big someday. Well, okay, ducks have big feet, too.

"Don't worry, *Abuela!*"

The life of a duck is pleasant. My head and shoulders are hot in the sun, my bottom and legs cool in the water. The maguey fibers I'm floating on fluff around me like a nest. My job is to push them under the water, to keep them wet. Settled comfortably, I paddle my feet gently, spreading my toes. This is the easiest job in the world.

Shading my eyes, making a frame with my fingers, I look across the water of the lagoon to the spit of land my grandparents farm. I frame their house made of sticks, thatched with dry leaves, lacy brown against the purple volcano. Abuela stands outside, a black and white rectangle in her semimournful dress. A stick fence to one side: that's the pigpen. A planting of maguey, spiky and blue-green. Around the house, sparse green grass, orange mud. Romy, in a short white dress, is feeding leaves to black chickens. From where I float, everything looks small, neat and complete. The kind of scene you could hang on the wall. Usulután, El Salvador, School Holidays. I want to hold it the way it is—*click!*—as if I had a camera.

I wave to Abuela, a big wave with my whole arm.

"Should I come in?" I trumpet through cupped hands.

"Not yet!" shouts my grandmother. "The twine has to soak longer!"

She calls it twine already, because that is what my nest will become. All morning she and my little sister Romelia and I have been stripping the fibers from maguey plants. Now I'm soaking the fibers, and when the fibers get soft enough in the water, we'll twist them into twine. Abuela trades the twine for things she needs at *Don* Ignacio's store—candles, rice, cough medicine.

It's fine with me to stay floating, dizzy in the sun. I scoop up cool water and drip it on my head, down my back.

When the sun lowers just a little, I'll come in. Romelia and I can begin twisting the twine. I want to be hard at work when my grandfather returns from his cornfield.

My grandfather Chuy usually comes home when the setting sun first touches the top of the volcano. Maybe, if we had a clock, it would be about five. I picture his machete hanging from his wrist, his digging stick over his shoulder. Sweat pours from under his hat into his eyes. His shirt sticks to his back. Sometimes he is so tired that he lurches like a drunk.

If Grandfather Chuy comes home and finds me playing duck, seeming to do nothing, I will be so embarrassed that I might as well just slip off down into the water, *blub blub,* and disappear forever.

Mama warned us.

"At your grandparents' you'll be lucky if you have time to scratch your nose," she said. "In the country, work is life."

We've been here a month this time. I know by the moon, which was small when we arrived and is small again now. My hands are tough and my arms have all kinds of muscles. I love work, but I worry about displeasing Grandfather Chuy, just because of something I overheard.

THE HOUSE has one room. My grandparents sleep separated from Romy and me only by a hanging blanket. I can't help overhearing their conversations; I lie awake a long time at night, especially when I'm sleeping in a hammock.

Our very first night here, I heard my grandfather talking to Abuela.

"Tell me what you think of our daughter's companion."

I held my breath, because it was my father Jacinto he was asking about.

"Well, Chuy," said the voice of Abuela Ana, floating from behind the blanket, "Jacinto is a dreamer, an idealist . . . honest, yes, and a good father. I only hope that he won't leave our daughter crying."

"She brought the children out to us because of danger in town. Did she tell you, Ana? Jacinto has been imprisoned twice already for political activities. . . ."

"Yes, Chuy, I know."

"You knew and didn't tell me?"

"It was over, Chuy. Why should I give you more worry?"

"It is not over, is it? He continues with the same work."

"That and his job of drawing pictures to build houses . . ."

I heard a snort from my grandfather. Not a mean laugh, but still . . . "Ana, how can holding meetings and drawing pictures be work? Truly. How can a man who doesn't sweat find favor with God?"

My grandmother answered something in a pleasant tone, but I couldn't hear the words. My heart was beating in my ears. I went to sleep planning ways to sweat when my grandfather was around.

Twisting twine, you get hot even when the sun is low.

I bend my arms like wings, scoop into the water, and begin paddling in.

THE SUN DROPS suddenly behind the tallest mountain. Night is here. At the door of the hut, Grandfather Chuy sits on the split-log bench and smokes his cigar. He is resting, thinking, talking to himself. Romy and I have worked hard on the twine. We've filled sixteen bobbins, each holding about twenty meters of twine. I write it down so that when Abuela goes to trade with *Don* Ignacio, she can tell him just how much is there.

"Look what he writes, Chuy!" says Abuela, showing him the paper. "Felipe's schooling is good." I can see by the light of her candle that she has tears in her eyes. "With such schooling, they'll never take this boy for the army," she says.

"True, they seem to want only illiterates for the army," says my grandfather.

I am surprised by the bitterness in his voice. Suddenly I remember that my mother's brothers, who grew up in this same house, were taken to serve in the army before I was born, and have never come back. My mother warned me not to speak of her brothers to Chuy or Abuela. I wonder about these boys, my young uncles, who have become nobody in their own family. An unspoken emptiness in the middle of normal conversation.

"Then how would the army know who can read?" Romy asks Chuy. I am busy projecting profits on twine and don't hear his answer.

Later, Abuela blows out the candle, and Romy and I climb into our hammocks. The door is open, and I can see the tip of Chuy's cigar glowing red in the dark. Abuela could trade the twine for tobacco, if she wants. Not quite a necessity, like corn, or salt, or water. You wouldn't die without tobacco. A luxury, then. "But it keeps us healthy," says Chuy. "It keeps away mosquitoes."

"Cigars frighten away sadness and melancholy, as well," Abuela adds.

The stars begin to come out. By moving my head, I make them wink through holes in the roof and between the sticks of the walls. From the mountain come the sound of crickets and the calls of night birds. My grandmother begins to sing:

"Hush, little baby,
Pumpkin head.
Coyote will eat you
If you don't go to bed."

ABUELA IS HAPPY to have children in the house again, I can tell. Of course, there are no babies. Even Romy is eight, a big girl. But I like hearing Abuela sing her untrue baby song. Still awake, I hear Romy scratching her feet.

Romy is not good in school the way I am. That is, she doesn't get good grades. Though she is smart at home, it's possible that she will have to repeat third grade. She daydreams, and she thinks beyond whatever question is asked to all the other questions it could possibly bring up. She and Grandfather Chuy are alike; they have their feet in the dirt, but their thoughts curl like smoke exploring the wind.

When Romy takes the pigs out of their pen to look for food, she talks and sings to them. She tickles their backs with a stick, herding them along toward the plants they like to eat. She searches for broom flowers, yellow and white, to feed to the pigs. And not just to the pigs. Romy eats flowers.

"Try them, Felipe," she says. "They are sweet-tasting and full of beauty."

"I am already full of beauty," I tell her, stretching. "Full of beauty and full of tortillas."

Romy smiles and shrugs. She goes barefoot, which Mama would not like, and gets chiggers in the bottoms of her feet from the pigs. At night her feet itch. She scratches them on the fibers of her hammock.

Abuela hears Romy, too. In the morning when Chuy has left to go work on the corn, she says, "Clean all the ashes from the stove, Romelia. Otherwise the Cipitio will come to play in the ashes and tickle your feet all night."

"Who is the Cipitio?" Romy asks.

"You don't know?" asks Abuela, surprised. "The one who tickles your feet!"

Romy opens her eyes wide in the light that filters through the roof. She shakes her head, her hair a black cloud.

"The Cipitio is a monster who likes to play in ashes," Abuela explains.

"Abuela," I say. "With all respect, we don't believe in stuff like that. Romy's feet itch because she has chiggers."

"You can believe and not believe," says my grandmother kindly. "But it will be good for Romelia to clean the stove ashes."

Romy begins to clean the stove, brushing the ashes onto a piece of tin and carrying them out to the corner of the pig yard, where the new trees have been planted.

She comes running back and stands panting, scratching the bottom of one foot against the side of her knee.

"Abuela, there is a man down by the ocotillos. He wants to talk to you."

Abuela is perfectly still for a moment, bent over her washing. Then she wipes her hands, straightens her black hair, and marches out to the back of the pen. Romy and I follow at a distance.

The man is a boy, really, just five or six years older than me, and hungry. He is barefoot. He carries his machete strapped to one wrist, and an empty canvas bag is slung over one shoulder.

"Tía," he says, "can you spare me some water? I can pay you."

"Water is holy," says Abuela, watching him steadily. "It is a sin to withhold it. A sin to sell it."

The young man nods and follows Abuela to the shallow well Chuy dug himself. The water in it is cleaner than in the lagoon, and doesn't carry disease. The well water is clear, with a taste of clay. I lower the bucket, pull it up easily, fill the man's canvas bag. The only sound is the slow trickle. Full, the bag must weigh fifteen kilos.

"Can you sell me some corn or millet?" asks the stranger.

We have dried corn stored in a jar. It hangs on a string from the roof pole so that mice won't get it. Abuela sells three scoops to the man, filling a plastic bag he pulls from his pocket.

"Go with God," she tells him, as he leaves the shade of the house.

Abuela's dog, Piri, follows the stranger away, sniffing his heels, and then comes back to us.

Until the dog returns, the three of us are quiet.

"Was he one of the *muchachos*?" I ask Abuela.

The *muchachos* are the guerrillas. We call them "guys" in a friendly way because they defend the peasants from the landowners and the military. The authorities call them something else: "subversives." A subversive sounds like a pest, a mouse or mole or maybe a termite. Something to be gotten rid of.

Abuela shrugs. "He was a dream, an apparition. You did not see him," she says. "Forget that he was here."

2

"Mazingers"

ANOTHER night stretches across the lagoon. The chickens are clucking gently on their branch in the mango tree. Romy and I swing like cocoons in our hammocks. Piri lies snoring on the ground below me, where I can dangle my hand to scratch his neck. Chuy and Abuela are on the bench in a cloud of cigar smoke, listening to crickets.

A coyote howls. *Go to sleep, pumpkin head.* A dog barks, then another. A chain of dogs, barking up the mountain. Piri sits up, alert and growling. In the hamlet and along the road that leads past the lagoon, everyone has dogs. For companionship. For warning. Chuy leans forward, puts out his cigar, stands up. Beneath the dogs' racket we begin to hear a low, grumbling sound.

"Trucks," says Abuela.

"Mazingers," says Chuy. Mazingers are big, heavily armored trucks. We have them in the city, too. They make a rumble that's like a bad dream or a stomachache. Romy jumps out of her hammock and comes to stand beside me.

"Felipe," Abuela says suddenly, "is there unused fiber still?"

"Yes, Abuela, a lot more."

"Run now. Push it out onto the lagoon. Quietly paddle with your hands across to the south, away from us, away from any lights they will shine. No matter what you hear, come back only long, long after the trucks leave."

I look at Chuy but can't see his face in the dark. "Go!" he says, and puts a hand on Romy's shoulder, drawing her to him.

I slip out into the night. It has grown very dark. I find the rolls of fiber, pale blobs down near the water.

Behind me, in the door of the house, I hear Abuela say, "Romelia, we must tell them that your brother has gone back to the city for his studies. He left yesterday, if they ask. Gather his clothes. We'll push them up in the thatch. . . ."

I AM on the water again. Feeling the way a duck must feel when foxes are prowling. The water is still warm, the stars too bright now. But the volcano throws its shadow across the lagoon, and there is mist rising from the water as the night gets colder. I wish it would become as thick as clouds to hide me. I wish I were very, very small and feathered.

The military must have a battery-powered megaphone. The voice I hear across the water is mixed with the barking of dogs. The same things are repeated over and over, as if by a robot:

"Everyone out of your houses. . . .

"Out of your houses.

"Put your hands over your heads.

"Everyone out!"

And then, mean but human: "No! You can't bring that! What do you think this is, a picnic?"

I drift out of earshot, kicking quietly under the water, far from the searchlights that shine out from shore. I hear the revving of motors, but I can't tell which way the trucks are headed.

Once I hear a shot that echoes around the mountains. The same shot, again and again.

The sky gets darker. The stars swell and pulse and reflect in the black water. I lose track of which way is up and which down. I chew my knuckles and pull my hair to stay awake. The fiber is soaked now. It barely floats, and I'm sinking lower and lower. Each time I jolt awake, the sky is a different color. At last, the stars grow dim; one by one they are going out.

DAWN AT LAST. Because of the light, it seems safe to paddle back. It is very far, and the maguey fibers that were as fluffy as clouds yesterday feel as hard and heavy as wire now. In the soft pink light creeping over the mountain, I find the familiar spit of land. My legs are so cold, they won't hold me. I crawl across the wet grass up to the house.

WHILE ABUELA rubs my legs to put back the feeling, Romy talks about the night visit of soldiers.

"They lined us up on the soccer field, Felipe. They had searchlights on top of the trucks, and they shined them in our eyes so that we couldn't see. They yelled at people through a cone that made their voices loud. . . ." Romy holds her hands up beside her ears like claws, shaking them. "Nobody could understand what they were saying. But Piri knew it was mean. See how fearful he is now? A soldier beat him with the butt of his gun."

"I heard a shot. . . ."

"That was Macario," says Abuela, still rubbing my legs. "He didn't want to hurry for the soldiers. He is old and has his pride. They shot his foot. . . ."

Romy breaks in. "When everybody was lined up on the soccer field, they pointed the light at people one by one. They stopped the light on three boys who were together, and jerked them out of the line. One of them fell on his hands and knees. 'You'll be lucky if the army will take you!' they said to him. 'Clumsy!' "

Grandfather Chuy sits on the bench, nodding at Romy's words, stroking Piri, who still has his tail between his legs.

"I was afraid. . . ." I begin, and stop. I don't know how to tell them how glad I am to see them there, alive. Abuela is standing behind me now, holding me across the shoulders. I put my hands over hers, feeling her wrinkly knuckles.

"Cat's luck, Felipe," says Chuy. "That's what you have. If you weren't quick, you'd be in the army now. A Salvadoran soldier."

"It wasn't just cat's luck—it was Abuela," I say.

"Isn't twelve too young for the army?" asks Romy.

"Not here. Not now," Abuela says. "Here in the country, we don't even want our children to have birthdays anymore."

ROMY IS SENT to *Don* Ignacio's store with a letter to put on the microbus when it comes through on its way to the city. The letter tells Mama and Jacinto what has happened.

Mama will come on the bus, we know. It will take her four days at least: two to get the message, and two to get off from work and to travel.

WE ARE WAITING at *Don* Ignacio's store when the bus arrives in a cloud of dust.

Mama jumps off, bouncing a string bag over her shoulder. She looks small, tight with energy. A big smile, but her face is pointy. She seems pale now that we've become so brown.

As the bus pulls away, we measure up, face-to-face. On tiptoe, I'm a half-centimeter taller than Mama is.

"Aha!" I have to tease her to make sure she is still herself.

Mama slowly winds her black braid into a knot and pins it on top of her head.

"Aha to you," she says, raising an eyebrow, and she pulls my ear.

Romy takes her bag, and we set off toward the lagoon.

"I HAVE TO TAKE them home," Mama says to Abuela Ana, to Chuy. "We might not be so lucky the next time. And if the authorities knew you had hidden Felipe . . . they would burn your house, Mamita, or worse."

Worse.

"Come with us, Abuela Ana. Come with us, Chuy," I say.

"Please!" begs Romy.

"Romelia," says Chuy. I can tell from the way he looks at her that she is as dear to him as his machete. "Do you think your grandfather could live in the city? Away from the lagoon? Away from the corn?"

"No," Romy answers truthfully. But I think of old Macario, Chuy's friend, with one foot shot off. And the way Chuy can suddenly become angry.

My father Jacinto is almost the same age as my grandfather Chuy. Romy doesn't believe this, but I figured it out and it's true.

What happened is this. When our mama, whose real name is Paloma, was thirteen years old, there was a famine in the country near the lagoon. Corn shriveled, there was nothing to eat, and people began to starve. A widow from there moved to town and found work. Because she was a good friend of Abuela Ana's, she found a position for Paloma, too. Even though Paloma was still young, by working in town she could send food home to her brothers. Paloma's job was to clean and cook for a bachelor who lived next door to where the widow worked.

The bachelor was an architecture student, Jacinto Ramirez. The way my father tells it, Paloma was beautiful and funny, and she distracted him from his studies. So he decided to teach her to read and write, so that she would be busy, too. Soon they became *compañeros*, companions for life. Paloma took Jacinto to the lagoon to meet her parents and brothers, and then they went back to town, and I was born.

Ever since I have known them, they have been planning their wedding.

Mama's name, Paloma, means "dove." I think her name has dignity. I like it. But almost nobody calls her Paloma, except Mama's parents. Jacinto and their friends in town call her Palomitas, which means "popcorn."

Jacinto doesn't act old. Okay. It is true that Jacinto doesn't sweat much, not nearly as much as Chuy, but this doesn't mean he's lazy. Jacinto wears clean shirts every day and drives a Honda motorcycle to work. And as for work, he sits in an office and draws big blue pictures for making buildings, thinking very hard. On the ceiling there is a fan that turns to keep him cool, lifting the edges of the paper. So what? Jacinto is great.

AT LAST the bus pulls up into the terminal, and there he is. Straddling his bike, in jeans and a light blue shirt with sleeves rolled up, with dark glasses on and a big smile.

"Jacinto!"

"Papa!"

"Chicos!"

We have a family reunion while our feet melt into the asphalt. We climb on the bike in our usual formation: Romy wedged sideways in front of Jacinto, Mama behind him, arms locked around his waist, and me behind her, hanging on for dear life to keep off the scalding muffler.

Jacinto revs up the engine. "This family is getting too big!" he shouts over the noise. "This is the last time, the absolutely last time, I take you all for a ride at once."

"Felipe!" Mama squeals as we go around a curve. "I can't breathe. Have mercy!" Because I have to hang on tight, or it's good-bye, Felipe.

"Do you want me to have the rear end of a baboon, Mama?" I ask her neck, to make her aware of the danger I'm in.

Jacinto grumbles about the flat tires he will have.

Romy looks perfectly comfortable, perched up front like a butterfly.

AFTER CHUY and Abuela's *rancho*, our house in Santa Tecla, with two rooms downstairs and another two up, looks suddenly tall. In front is our yard, fenced with sticks that we painted blue. Squash flowers bloom orange and yellow all over the fence. Romy's chickens put up a big squawk when Jacinto drives the bike in through the gate, almost scraping my knees off. Home! Our dog, Payaso, jumps up on me and knocks me off the bike before it stops.

Mama brings lemonade to the tin table in the yard. Jacinto asks us a million questions about

Chuy and Abuela, about pigs and crops, about *Don* Ignacio and the twine business. He even asks the names of the boys who were taken by the army, but we don't know. I wish that the time could go on and on, but Jacinto is called to the phone at a neighbor's, and Mama and Romy go to take a nap.

ENRIQUE IS my good friend in town. Even if I am sad to have left Abuela and Chuy, it's okay with me, because now I can get together with Enrique and practice soccer. I've always been a fast runner, and finally this summer I've learned to control the ball. I have strategy. I can plan ahead and make things happen in the game.

In the late afternoon, Enrique and I meet in a vacant lot. When we can get teams together, we move some broken blocks around for goals. Enrique and I are usually the captains. When it's just us, we keep the weeds down by running laps around the edges of the field.

Our part of town is up on the mountain, and you can see the city of San Salvador, red and dusty, down below, blue mountains behind it. Enrique and I run, racing in spurts of speed. Every once in a while we jump into the air for the stretch.

Payaso chases us until I yell at him for tripping me. Then he goes off nosing.

SOMETIMES people dump stuff in the lot, so I don't pay much attention when I see Payaso fussing with a bone. But Enrique runs over with a strange look on his face.

"Take a look at what your dog has found," he says.

I look. I see it. What Payaso is holding in his teeth is part of a man's arm and hand.

I scream at Payaso, and he drops it. I get cold and sweaty, and when I look around, Enrique is gone. I take off my shirt and use it to grab the thing, and once I've wrapped it up, I feel better. I don't know what to do, so I take it home.

MAMA AND ROMY are out. Jacinto is in the yard, working on his bike. He has a cloth on the ground, and valves and pistons are laid out on it in a neat row. Jacinto is cleaning off carbon carefully, with sandpaper. It's getting dark. I know he wants to finish working. I don't know what to tell him. I have the strangest feeling that the minute I open my mouth, the whole world will change. I stick the bundle in the orange tree and go and get another shirt. Then I squat down beside Jacinto.

"Still in shape?" he asks.

"Hmm."

"Fast as Enrique?"

"Hmm."

Jacinto turns around at last.

"Felipe! Are you sick?"

And I am, all over the ground.

Jacinto gets a wet rag to wipe my face. He gets a drink of water for me so I can rinse my mouth. He puts an arm around my shoulders, and after a while he says, "What happened, Felipe?" So I tell him.

"Shouldn't we bury it?" I ask.

Jacinto shakes his shoulders as if to chase away a ghost. "Let me take it down to the Human Rights Office first, Felipe."

"Why?"

"They can maybe still get a fingerprint. For identification. Someone might need to know."

"What . . ."

"What it was doing there. Probably political murder, son. Someone who dared to speak out against the government. The death squads often dismember."

Jacinto gives a big sigh and ruffles my hair. His hand is warm and strong and alive. "Let's clean up," he says.

BY THE TIME Mama and Romy come home, Jacinto and I have raked the yard clean, my shirt is washed and flapping on the clothesline, and Jacinto has wrapped and hidden the hand.

Romy and Mama are in a good mood.

"Sorry we're so late, *chicos*!" says Mama. "And I hope you are hungry, because we have brought you a delicious supper."

Jacinto puts his hand on the back of my neck and gives me a shake, for courage.

"Qué bueno!" he says. "Great!"

4

Summer in the City

SUMMER GOES ON. We aren't allowed on the vacant lot anymore. "I'm sorry, *chicos*, but . . ." Enrique and I are allowed to practice soccer on two streets, his or mine, not beyond. And only after certain hours, when most of the women have their shopping done, so we won't knock people down. Between dawn and three, I stay home with Romy. She is allowed to have two friends over but is forbidden to go out on the street until Mama comes home and can go with her.

ROMY AND I play a lot of hopscotch in the yard. We groom the chickens until they shine. We've built a platform in the orange tree.

In the evening, the beautiful evening, Mama, Jacinto, Romy, and I sit outside in the cool of the yard. Now that I'm as tall as Mama, I decide to try calling her by her real name, Paloma, though it doesn't come naturally. Paloma likes to climb up the orange tree and sit on the platform with Romy, dangling her feet and telling us stories about the shrimp plant where she works, where all the women stand at tubs, heading and cleaning shrimps to freeze for export.

"What terrible gossips you are," says Jacinto, laughing up at Paloma. "Tell us more."

"We have to gossip to keep our fingers warm," Paloma says. "Romy, please don't tell a word of this to your friends. Only some of it is made up!"

"Ah, but which part?" wonders Jacinto.

Some nights, Jacinto lets me oil and help tune his bike, while he explains to me how everything goes together. The mysteries of the internal-combustion engine. Bernoulli's principle.

SOME NIGHTS, people come over to see Jacinto. In ones and twos, they slip quietly through the gate, letting themselves in with soft, friendly greetings, shadowy in the moonlit yard. When they arrive, Romy and I are sent to bed. We would like to stay, but we are not even introduced.

One night, late, after the visitors have gone, I hear Mama and Jacinto talking as they come upstairs.

"What if they come for you, as they did for Umberto?"

"Say that we fought. Say I moved away to live with another woman."

"But what if you are here?"

"Aie, Palomitas, then I'll just have to go, won't I?"

"And if they take us both?"

"Rafa will look after the children."

"Would they . . . ?"

"Take the children? Yes, love, they might. To get me to talk. Don't cry. Listen: if they come for me, you and the children grab hands and run. Go north, all the way to Canada. If ever I get free, I'll go there and . . ."

Their door closes, and their voices become so gentle that I can't hear. Tears run down the sides of my face. Into my ears, onto my pillow.

THE NEXT MORNING, I wake hoping that their conversation was a dream. But I look up Canada in Jacinto's map book, in case it wasn't. Canada stretches across the top of North America like Heaven on a hopscotch game. It is very big, and very close to the Arctic.

"JACINTO," I whisper one evening when we are alone out in the yard. I want to tell him that I overheard their conversation. Different words come.

"If I'm old enough to be wanted by the army, don't you think I'm old enough to understand what you do?"

Jacinto holds a lug nut in one hand and polishes it for a long time.

"You are right, Felipe," he says at last. "You are old enough now. Smart enough, tough enough. . . ." He hesitates, leaving me glowing with the compliments. "But—do you want everything that goes with knowing? Do you want to have to decide? I myself don't always know what is right to do. . . ."

I'm not sure I really want him to talk about his work. I only want him to talk to me. I know that Jacinto hopes my ignorance will be a protection against torture. That's why he doesn't introduce me to his visitors. Not because I am unimportant.

I can see that Jacinto is about to drift into one of his melancholy moods, so I ask him how to put the timing chain back on the bike.

ONE AFTERNOON, practicing soccer, Enrique kicks the ball crazily to get around my block, and it hits an old lady. She isn't hurt, but the apologies take time. We dust her off. We get her a cup of water. We collect her groceries, and Enrique goes and buys two more eggs to replace the ones that are broken. We stand in the sun because she seems cold. Finally she stops shaking. We make her agree that we are, after all, good boys.

It's hot in our yard. I'm happy to open the door to the house, which is built of concrete blocks and is always shady and cool. I see a piece of paper stuck under the door, just inside. I pick it up.

"Mama! Paloma! I'm home." She always wants to know, even if she's taking a shower out back in the washhouse.

Paloma doesn't answer. And Romy's not around, either. Maybe they're out together. I read the note while I'm going for a glass of water. The handwriting is clumsy. Bigger and shakier than Romy's.

LEAVE AND DON'T COME BACK. IF NOT, <u>YOU</u> DIE.

I wonder why they put the line under "you." I lean my forehead against the watercooler. There is nothing on the other side of the note. It's not addressed to anyone.

I'M SHIVERING. I want to be back in the sun. I sit on the step and try to forget about the paper. I make a circle in the dust of the yard and flip pebbles into it. The pebbles are warm. Fear is making a hole in my brain. The paper under the door is in the middle of it. I can't forget about it, and I can't think about it, either.

At last Romy comes home. I love how normal she looks, trying to sneak in quietly at the gate. When she sees me, she freezes, her eyes big.

"Is Mama back yet?" she whispers.

"No, I don't know. I just came in. . . . Where were you?"

"I had to go see Emilia, only for a minute, to tell her to come over. It's boring being so cooped up all the time."

I don't show Romy the note. We feed the chickens and let them out of their pen so they can peck around. While the chickens take dust baths, I wrestle with Payaso to keep him from chasing them. With my face buried in my dog's prickly fur, tickling his belly and growling along with him, I almost manage to forget the message.

PALOMA comes into the yard, banging the gate. She sees Romy, lets out a shout, and bursts into tears. She pulls Romy and me into such a bone-crunching hug, I think my head might pop off.

"Mama, we're not shrimps!"

Paloma drops down on the step, puts her hands over her eyes. Her shoulders shake, and for a second I hope she's laughing. But tears spurt out between her fingers.

"I asked everybody in the world!" she says between sobs. "Nobody knew where you were!"

Then she suddenly jumps to her feet. Her face is streaked and misshapen. Seeing her so scared, it is as if the ground has opened up under my feet. She runs inside the house, up the stairs two at a time, gallops back down, carrying Jacinto's belt. The one he never wears. She starts hitting Romy with it very hard, again and again.

"Never walk in the street alone! Never leave this house without my permission! You are a big girl now. There are bad men in the streets. Something terrible will happen to you! Then you will understand! Then you will be sorry!"

Romy doesn't hear any of what Mama says, because she is crying so hard and because she has her fingers in her ears.

Mama is not cruel. I've never seen her this way.

She gets plenty mad at us sometimes, for good reasons. But not crazy-mad like this.

JACINTO IS AWAY. His work sometimes takes him to construction sites; his absence is not so unusual. But he didn't tell us he was going, and he's been away for three days. After Romy has stopped crying and is in bed, Rafa, a friend of Jacinto's who works at the same office, comes by to see Paloma. They talk in the yard, but when I come out of the house, they are suddenly quiet.

MAMA TELLS ME that Jacinto's motorcycle has been found outside the city, not wrecked but abandoned.

I DON'T SHOW Mama the paper; I just leave it facedown on the table. The wording makes me afraid for Jacinto. Now I'm afraid for Mama, too. I hope she won't find the note just yet. Not until she feels better. But when will that be? Only when Jacinto comes home safe.

I think *I* will feel safer when she finds the note. Paloma is brave. She won't break. She'll know what to do.

5

Fast Forward

PALOMA HAS FLOWN into action. It's a big relief to see her making decisions, not crying. Romy and I don't dare ask her what it's all leading up to. Mama is like a balloon about to burst, a volcano ready to explode.

Paloma gives orders. We scurry to obey.

"Felipe! The neighbors need you to help build a chicken coop."

"Come with me, Romy, so that I don't die of nerves waiting in line at the bank."

"*Chicos*! You'll have supper with Rafa tonight. I'm going over to the church to talk with Father Gustavo."

"Take these pots to *Doña* Lidia, Felipe! She can use some new cook pots. . . . And yes! Those baby clothes, too. Give them to Serena."

"Romy! Let me see those shoes! Wiggle your toes. Are you sure they are big enough?"

Coming in from an errand down the street, I find Paloma sitting on my bed. Her mouth is clamped shut on a row of pins. With scissors she is opening up the seams around the top of my favorite pants. I watch in amazement. Beside her is a big pile of money. One by one, Paloma rolls up bills. One by one, she pokes them inside the tunnel where the elastic runs, pushing the money into the waistband. Some of the bills are Salvadoran *colones.* Some are *quetzales,* Guatemalan money. Some are green dollars such as the *yanquis* use.

Here's my chance to ask questions, but I'm afraid I'll make Mama swallow a pin. She takes them out of her mouth at last and, patting the waistband bulging with money, says, "Forget it's there." As if I could.

"Mama?"

"Yes, *chico.*"

"We're going, then?"

She nods.

"To Canada?"

"If we can make it."

"And—Jacinto?"

Paloma stands up jerkily, gathers her sewing things. "Jacinto is"—she hesitates—"here somewhere. We don't know where. Rafa looks for him every day. Other friends, too. He said—" Paloma tightens up all over, and her voice quavers, as if it might suddenly rise to a shriek.

"He said we should go to Canada. He'll meet us there," I finish for her. Paloma looks at me, pretends to inspect her sewing job. Her hands are shaking. Gradually she gets control of her face.

Without a word, Paloma and I are making an agreement. She will act normal if I agree not to ask about Jacinto.

Still I have to try:

"Is there any other way?"

Mama shakes her head without saying anything. I turn to go downstairs to tell Romy.

"No," I hear Mama say at last, behind my back, as if she were arguing with someone.

IF YOU ARE USED to being a certain kind of person, it's not so impossible to keep on being that person, even when you don't feel like it.

Mama calls me back, grabs me by the hair, and gives me a big smooch. She whispers in my ear, "Don't lose your pants, boy!"

"Ah!" I say. "The burdens of the rich." I say it to let her know that I understand the agreement. I'm proud that I can make a joke.

JUST FOUR DAYS LATER, at the time we should be starting back to school, Romy and I stand with Paloma and a suitcase, waiting for the bus that goes north.

Our neighbor Beatriz waits with us, leaning against the bus-stop sign. She has a smile on her face, but her eyes are red from crying. She babies Romelia, rocking and hugging her, arranging a bow on the top of her hair.

"We'll take good care of Payaso," Beatriz promises. "He will live like a king, as always."

Payaso is tied back in our yard, howling. Beatriz and her children are moving into our house because ours is bigger than theirs.

"And the chickens?" asks Romy. "You won't eat . . . ?"

"Like princesses," Beatriz assures her.

I can't believe that this is happening, that the bus will come and we'll just go.

"Mama . . ."

Paloma suddenly pulls a blanket out of our suitcase and runs across the road with it to a neighbor's house.

RAFA COMES AROUND the corner. I almost strangle with hope and dread. Then I see his face. He hasn't found Jacinto. Rafa holds me by the shoulders and leans over so that we are face-to-face. His eyes are dark and bloodshot and too solemn. I want to wriggle away. We have an agreement, I want to say. Say something funny, Rafa. Pretend it's okay.

"I will do everything in my power, Felipe, to find your father, my friend Jacinto."

Then Rafa, who is as big as a gorilla, starts sniffling. I stoop and retie the laces on my sneakers. Watching my fingers make a double knot, pressing my knee against my chest, I know Rafa doesn't have much hope of finding Jacinto alive.

But he has some. He has to have some.

Rafa blows his nose. I stand up and lean against his side so that I don't have to look at his face. He puts his arm around me, his hand on my shoulder.

We look around for Mama. If she doesn't get back before the bus comes, we won't have to go.

Just then, she shows up. Rafa gives her a hug that lifts her off the ground, and then, embarrassed, he runs off to work. He wouldn't take Jacinto's motorcycle, though Mama tried to lend it to him.

ENRIQUE COMES to the bus stop in his school clothes. We pass the time wrestling. When the bus pulls up, Enrique has me in a headlock, upside down. When he lets go, my ears are red and ringing. If Enrique says any famous last words, I don't hear them.

I KNOW THE BUS. It passes every week, smelling of burning motor oil and diesel fumes. It's rusty and full of dents. Above the windshield is painted the slogan *Baila, Mi Amor,* Dance, My Love. It's already packed with travelers from the city, and the driver sends us up to the roof to sit with the baggage. Just as Mama and I pull Romy onto the top of the bus, it lurches forward. By the time I catch my balance, we've turned a corner. Enrique is gone.

There's no time to think or worry, because it's so hard to stay on the roof. There are ten other people up top, using their bundles for cushions. Everyone hangs on to the baggage racks. The bus hits a pothole; people shout and grab us. I almost want to bounce off.

A peasant woman gives us a big burlap sack of corn husks to sit on. Paloma is so grateful that she unfastens our suitcase and gives the woman a blouse. The woman accepts it with protests—"No, no, no! It is nothing"—blushing with pleasure.

Farther along, a man throws on some bags of grain, and he invites me to lie against them. With my head sticking up in the wind, I watch the countryside flying past. Already, there's nothing familiar.

Baila's horn sounds no louder than the bleating of a goat, but people scatter when we roll past. Chickens dart for safety. Sounds loom up loud and fade just as quickly: the blare of a radio, the shouts of children meeting in the schoolyard. The *pop pop pop* of a motorcycle. Romy and I crane our necks over the edge of the roof, hoping. But it's not Jacinto. The man riding the motorcycle is some creep we've never seen.

THERE'S SOMETHING in the road that looks like a log. The driver swerves around it. I see that it's a body, a woman's body, I think, long dead. The driver doesn't stop.

"Did she get hit by a car?" Romy asks.

"Maybe," says Paloma.

"The military, the *escuadrones*, throw people they've killed in the road to make it look like a traffic accident," the peasant woman explains to Romy in a matter-of-fact voice. "You'll see more," she adds. People stop talking and look at the woman with pity and respect. They seem to think she's crazy to be so outspoken. *The death squads often dismember,* I hear Jacinto say, and try not to think of his motorcycle with no one on it. I squint my eyes half-shut, watching the clouds go by.

Romy has tears streaming from her eyes. She puts her head close to Mama's, the wind whipping their hair. I lean over, too, to hear what they're saying.

"When do we get to Canada?" Romy asks.

"Shhh . . . ," says Paloma. "That place is half a world away from here."

For a moment, Mama looks frightened. Then she pulls Romy over and tickles her.

"How do you like air travel, *chica*?" Paloma asks.

THERE ARE SOME crinkling sounds coming from around my waist, but no one will hear in all this noise of wind and wheels. Paloma has money, too, hidden somewhere. On a thong around her neck, she wears a packet with a letter from Father Gustavo, our birth certificates, and her identification card.

Before we left home, she drilled us on her rules for traveling until we could tick them off on our fingers:

Avoid the authorities.
Be polite.
Let Mama do the talking.
Like a chameleon, blend in wherever you are.

Paloma says we will travel mostly by bus and sometimes on foot. Father Gustavo gave her a list of churches where people might let us stay. She knows it by heart. The names of villages and priests make a chant she can say in less time than a Hail Mary in the Rosary. She drilled us on that, too, in case we get separated. She decided not to write the names. Whatever people have against you, the authorities or the *muchachos*, it doesn't do any good to mix up others in it.

ALL DAY AND NIGHT and the next day, too, we bounce through valleys and around volcanoes, past coffee plantations, over rivers, through villages. In some we stop, and sometimes a woman selling food raises her tray of tortillas and salt or sections of sugarcane up to us, and we hand down money to her. So we aren't hungry.

The driver pulls over out in the country, near bushes, for a relief stop. Then he honks three times, and people come running from the bushes to hop back on the bus, buttoning up their pants. Romy and I chase each other in circles around the bus. *Honk!* Back on the bus! The driver takes off while I am still only halfway up the ladder. I hang on, and a man on top pulls me up. People laugh and slap me on the back.

We come into an area where there are no crops in the fields. Weeds have taken over. Signs of fire and bombing are everywhere. The trees are in shreds. The houses that are still standing have burn marks and caved-in roofs. The only thing we see alive is a goat, nosing around in a burned-out house. A bunch of buzzards circle. I don't look closely. I don't want to see more bodies.

No one comes to the road when the driver honks, so he steps on the gas and hurries on.

THE BUS SIGHS to a stop in the plaza of a town up in the mountains. Paloma says, "This is it, *chicos*. Bye-bye to *Baila*."

We are very stiff. Before we can get up, the bus driver climbs onto the roof and throws all of the cargo—bags of seed and cabbages, bundles, and even chickens—down to the people below. He doesn't look where he is throwing, and he curses when somebody drops something. A man stumbles and falls, trying to catch a bag of cabbages. The bus driver laughs. I look at Paloma.

"Why did he laugh?"

"Because the one who fell is a peasant and an Indian," she whispers to me.

"Abuela is a peasant and an Indian," I whisper to Mama.

She nods. "Me, too," she says, and rubs my neck.

"And Chuy," I say.

"And you . . . ," Mama whispers.

"Oh!" I look at Mama. I think she means it.

We say good-bye to the people we've been traveling with and climb down the ladder. My legs are wobbly. Or the ground is moving.

The authorities patrol the square. Teenage boys in uniform, wearing dark glasses, holding automatic rifles. Mama squeezes our shoulders as we pass them, and says clearly:

"Take heart, *chicos*! Just a few more steps to Abuela's."

We have no Abuela here. Paloma is fooling the authorities.

TAKING HEART is even harder on the ground than it was on top of the bus. Sadness sweeps over me like a big wave. I look at Mama. She moves stiffly, like a puppet, but she is wearing the same slightly worried expression she always has when she is looking for a place to buy a cheap sandwich. She is pretending to be normal. Seeing this makes me remember our agreement and gives me a clue how to act. I begin to make my own rules for traveling:

> Act younger.
> Think less.
> Play and run.
> Don't wonder about Payaso.
> Imagine Jacinto alive.

"Race you to that ceiba tree!" I call to Romy. We run on legs as wobbly as cooked macaroni. We fall against the tree, complaining of the pins and needles in our feet.

6

The Madman of Guija

THERE'S A BREEZE in this town that feels as if we're on the edge of the sea. The trees whisper in the wind, and the wind smells of fish. We are on the edge of the Lago de Guija. The lake is shared by El Salvador and Guatemala. The three of us sit on a rock, soaking our feet, looking out over the water.

"A border is—nothing, just a line on a map between countries," Paloma explains to Romy. "But in the minds of the authorities, a border is as real as a rock."

"Yes, but what will it look like?"

"On the ground some borders are marked with barbed wire, some with water, and in some places they are not marked at all. And if you don't have papers stamped in all the right places, the authorities don't let you cross a border."

Romy sighs.

"I'll tell you when I see one, Romy," I say. Maybe I'm looking at one right now. Paloma must have a reason for bringing us this way. A lake along a border is hard for authorities to patrol.

ROMY AND I run in the park by the bus stop, and Mama walks around the square. People are coming out for their evening stroll, but they don't pay any attention to us. We look like everybody else. Romy coaxes a pigeon to eat leaves out of her hand.

Mama calls us, and we go to an open-air tavern. Romy and I sit at a table. "Stay here," Mama says, and goes up to the bar. She buys us tortillas, tomatoes, and orange drinks. While we eat, Paloma goes back and talks to the woman behind the bar.

The woman looks around to see if anyone is listening. Only me. Quickly, I look the other way and yawn. It's not hard to do. The woman motions Paloma closer and whispers something to her. I watch through watery eyes. Paloma pulls some bills from her pouch. She hands them to the woman. The woman puts them down her shirt.

She checks her cooking and then calls a boy from the kitchen and says a few words to him. The boy leaves the tavern.

Paloma comes back to our table. "She says we must wait," she tells us softly, "and there is an outhouse in the back."

WE SIT QUIETLY for a long time at our corner table. Mama shakes me out of sleep, and I'm disgusted to find that my face is stuck to the table. I try to scrub my cheek with the bottom of my shirt.

The boy is back. He leads us out of the tavern and down a dark street away from the square. The night is chilly and damp. Romy is stumbling with sleepiness. Mama wraps her shawl around Romy's shoulders and pushes her along like a sleepwalker. I have the suitcase and the bag of corn husks, which I sling over my shoulder in a way that I hope looks natural. I try to keep my eyes on the boy so we won't lose him. I have to watch my feet, too, so I won't trip. I wish the boy would slow down, or that I knew where I was going.

He turns into an alley, and we follow after him. The ground becomes boards. I see something shining on the ground and realize with a

start that it's the moon's reflection on water. It's
a dock we're on, not a street. The water stretches
so far that you can't see the other side. It moves
in big, slow, dark waves.

The boy is silhouetted in the light of a kero-
sene lantern at the end of the dock. As we get
nearer, I see moths and sausage bugs flying
around the lantern, flinging themselves against
the glass. Some get inside and sizzle.

The boy speaks into the darkness. "Uncle?
Uncle? I brought the passengers. Uncle?"

"Quiet!" says a deep voice. It comes from the
shadow of a boathouse at the end of the dock.
A man steps out suddenly, silently. He has on a
leather hat and a gray serape. He smells of fish
and sour tequila, and his eyes in the lantern light
are red and wild. Romy draws closer to Mama.
The man's voice comes out in short growls.

"You want to go across? You have money? You
better have money. It's dangerous on the lake.
Patrol boats. I don't risk my skin for nothing.
You give me three hundred *colones*. Now!"

I hear Paloma's breath catch.

"So much!" she says. "*Hombre*, we have far to
go. Many borders to cross."

"Three hundred it is. Or you swim. You can
swim, can't you, little one?"

With a gnarled, fishy hand, he reaches out for Romy's chin. Romy disappears into Mama's shawl.

"Can you, big boy?"

People call me "big" only to make fun of me.

The man reaches toward me. I want to be home in my bed. Not balancing on shaking legs on this rickety dock. Not here with this wild, drunken man and the dark, dangerous water under our feet. No, I can't swim. Paddle, sure, but not swim.

I can feel Mama's anger without looking at her. Paloma turns away from the light and takes money from her clothes.

"Take us across, then."

She agrees without a fight! I want to go back.

We step cautiously into an open boat. There's no motor, only long oars, and rags are wrapped around the oarlocks. Very quietly, the man rows us out onto the lake. Very quietly, we cross, hearing sounds from the town getting fainter and fainter, straining our eyes watching for patrol boats. Sometimes the man spits over his shoulder into the lake.

Romy is crouched beside me on a board that runs across the rowboat. Her hand makes its way into mine. Her nails are chewed low, and the ends of her fingers are bald and calloused.

THE OTHER SIDE of the lake is closer now than the one we left. We can't see any village on this side, but we hear voices up on the shore. It's hard to tell how far away they are. We come to the mouth of a creek, where cottonwood trees grow thickly. With a long sigh, the bow of the rowboat digs into a soft sand. Two almost invisible forms appear out of the darkness and pull the boat farther up onto the shore.

"Get out now," the rower says. His voice is low and full of caution. We stand unsteadily and pick our way across the bottom of the boat. We step down into damp sand. The man is close behind us.

"You pay now."

"But I paid you! Remember? Three hundred *colones* I paid you!" Mama whispers urgently, her voice rising.

"That was on the other side. Here I have to pay these others. Come on, three hundred more, or we tell the police you crossed the border illegally!"

A dog barks somewhere through the trees. We see the headlights of a car or truck moving on a road nearby.

"You can't do this! We'll have no money to continue."

"All right, you can complain to the soldiers."

The man pulls out a shiny whistle from under his serape. It dangles from his neck on a string. He fingers it a moment and then puts it in his mouth while we watch, frozen with fear.

"No, wait!" Paloma reaches into her pouch once again and counts out more dark bills. The man strikes a match, looks at them quickly, and shakes the match out. He approaches the other two and gives a bill to each of them. He grins at us, still holding the whistle between his teeth. Then he lets it drop. I can see his teeth in the dark, but not his eyes.

He climbs into his boat, and the two other men shove the boat off the bank. He pulls away from the shore on his silent oars and vanishes into the darkness. Just as suddenly, the other men slip away, and we are alone.

7

Father Ramón's Children

"WELL," SAYS PALOMA. "Welcome to Guatemala."

She kisses us each on both cheeks. "Somebody should make a ceremony," she says.

Then we learn Paloma's fifth rule of travel: when in doubt, walk.

First we follow a sandy path that glows faintly in the dark. It smooths out into dark pavement, with holes that are hard to see. Looking up, I'm amazed by the brightness of stars. The moon has set. I think of Abuela.

We are under the same sky.

I step in a hole and twist my ankle. Mama takes the suitcase.

Just before light, we come to an abandoned warehouse with a sign for a bus stop. Paloma trudges by. Sleepwalking.

"Mama . . . ?"

"If we ride a bus so close to the border, they will question us."

"Who?"

"Guatemalan authorities."

We walk on, discouraged.

"Today is a chameleon day. Today we walk and hide."

IT ISN'T QUITE light yet, and there's a pink haze over everything. I touch my face to make sure I exist. It's there, clammy and cold. A few trees stand low and still against the ground, gray against pink. I keep checking to be sure they're really trees: they seem to be watching us.

"What will the authorities do if they find us, Mama?" Romy asks.

"I don't know, *chica*. I don't want to find out."

Paloma mumbles under her breath the litany of village names, priest names. "Father Ramón, in the town of Hondo. That's who we need to find. Tomorrow we'll catch a bus to Hondo."

"Father Ramón, Father Ramón," I repeat to myself over and over in time to my steps. One after the other, my feet hit the road, sending up puffs of dust. Sleep is overpowering me. "Father Ramón, Father Ramón, Father . . ."

I hear a rattle in the sky, can't think what it is. Mama drags us toward one of the low trees, pushes us under. A helicopter clatters over. I sink down on the sack of corn husks, dive down, down into sleep.

HILLS AND MOUNTAINS, each one steeper than the last. Romy needs better shoes. Walking behind her, I can see sores rubbing through her socks at the back of her heels. She doesn't say anything. I think about the map on the wall at school. We are walking right up the *cordillera*, the mountain range that runs between the seas, the backbone of Central America. I tell Romy, and she smiles faintly. "Each hill is a vertebra?" The backbone is very, very long.

We walk and nap, walk and nap, until I lose track of the time of day or night. In morning sun we're sitting on grass near the edge of the road, and Paloma is showing Romy how to rub out leg cramps when a bus comes barreling around the bend from behind us. Above the windshield, painted in big red letters, is its name: *Jesús Te Ama*, Jesus Loves You. This is enough to convince Paloma. She jumps up, flags the bus, and we clamber on board.

Jesús Te Ama drags itself uphill like a wounded turtle, zips downhill like a lizard. After so much walking, the hard benches make a change. Romy slips to the floor, asleep with her head bouncing on Mama's knee.

Even on a map, the roads in the *cordillera* wriggle like snakes. What the school map didn't show is that in many places the roads are washed out altogether.

Suddenly the bus screeches to a halt. Everyone gets out. The roof passengers climb down. Everyone stands along the edge of the washout, looking down at the slide of mud, the uprooted trees, the valley far, far below.

We look up at the tiny ledge of road that's left clinging to the rock face. You can see roots poking through the ledge of asphalt. There is no way it can be strong enough to hold a bus. Some young men are laughing and placing bets: will the bus make it? The driver has a gold tooth and a devil-may-care attitude. He takes a cigarette from his shirt pocket, smooths it, sticks it between his lips. To my surprise, he reaches inside the bus, pulls loose the steering wheel, and lights his cigarette on a wire inside the steering column. I think of what Jacinto would say: *Must be a bad connection if the wire's that hot, Felipe.*

I wish Jacinto himself would come walking up behind me, and not just the idea of him.

The young men cheer the bus driver, who crosses himself, waves jauntily, and takes off at top speed toward the ledge. As he hurtles across it, Romy covers her eyes. Mama chews her rosary. I watch. Pieces of asphalt fly. The bus seems suspended in midair. Then it crunches onto solid road beyond the break. All the passengers cheer as the driver comes out and takes a bow. We grab our bundles and, in careful single file, follow the bus.

"HONDO!" shouts the driver. We get off the bus with everyone else, look at the bridge that leads north across the river Motagua. Even though it isn't anywhere near a border, soldiers are asking people for papers. In the plaza a woman cries and shouts. She is being pushed by two young soldiers onto a bus. The soldiers are laughing. The woman's children stand by, embarrassed. I look away.

Paloma pays no attention to the commotion in the square. She wanders down a side street and ducks into a fruit shop. Inside, in the shade, she takes on the look of a housewife shopping. She feels the mangoes, looking for one that is just right, and sizes up the people who enter the shop.

An old lady with a gentle face comes in, greeting the shopkeeper by name. As she leans over the baskets of fruit to pick out a lemon, a wooden cross dangles from her neck.

"I wish I knew where to find Father Ramón," Mama says quietly, as if to me.

The woman glances up, looks us over slowly. "When we have bought our fruit, I can take you to Father Ramón," she says. "I am his cook, Josefina." A miracle.

THAT IS HOW we end the day in the kitchen of Josefina, helping her prepare supper for a yard full of people. Refugees. It's a word we hear more and more. That's what they call all people who have to leave their homes on account of war. Refugees, or fugitives. People on the run.

A boy my age named Nestor tells me that he is Father Ramón's assistant. "Because I am now on my own," he says.

"And where is the rest of your family, then?" I ask without thinking. We are squatting in the courtyard, drawing designs in the dust with sticks.

"We were on a bus," Nestor explains. "I was on top because it was so hot inside. But all the others—my mother and father, my brothers and sisters, my grandfather and my baby cousin Pascua—they were all inside. The authorities stopped the bus and killed them all with machine guns."

I am so shocked I drop the stick I'm drawing with, but Nestor keeps drawing, and he keeps talking, too.

"They sprayed the top of the bus with machine-gun fire, but I was behind some bags of seed, and nothing hit me. Later, after the soldiers had gone, some people brought me to Father Ramón."

Another boy here, Pablito, was burned by the phosphorus the military drops on trees. His skin looks like a map in brown and white. He is blind in one eye, so that we can't play soccer. We try hopscotch, but his balance isn't good. He is happier hauling water for Josefina, so I help him do that.

While we are in the kitchen, Father Ramón comes in. He looks like a cherub, with round pink cheeks and a big smile.

"Welcome, little daughter!" he says to Romelia, opening his arms for a hug. Romy runs right to him, and he hugs her and blesses her. He shakes my hand and rests his hand on my head. He takes Mama's hands, which she has quickly wiped on her apron, in both of his. "God bless you," he says. "I am happy that you have arrived in our house."

Another little girl comes in, a child with big dark eyes, younger than Romy. Father Ramón opens his arms to her and speaks gently, but at the sight of him she begins to scream and fastens herself around a leg of the table. Her screams are terrible, and no one can stop them.

Father Ramón looks so upset that I follow him out into the courtyard.

"Why does she scream, *Padre*?" I ask him. "Can I help?"

"Ask the soldiers why she screams, son," says Father Ramón. I have never heard anyone sound so sad.

I go to the corner of the courtyard. The girl is still crying, and everyone else is quiet. I pick up some pebbles, and some flowers that have fallen off the purple vines that grow around the courtyard. I give them to Romy in the kitchen.

"Take them to that little girl and see if she will play. You can make pictures."

Romy goes over and sits under the table next to the little girl. Slowly people in the kitchen start talking again. Romy arranges the flowers and pebbles in a face on the ground. The little girl watches. Her sobs slow down, hiccup, stop. After a while she reaches out and moves a pebble.

8

Deep River

"THE BRIDGE at Hondo is a trap, Palomita," Josefina reminds Mama anxiously. "Stay away from there." Josefina is up before dawn to make us coffee.

We've rested for two days, and Paloma thinks we need to move on. I have begged to stay here. We could make ourselves useful helping Father Ramón and Josefina. From here we could go back and look for Jacinto. From here we could still find our way home.

"We are going to Canada, Felipe," says Paloma in a sure voice, trying to convince herself.

"Walk east," Josefina urges us. "Find a boat. Don't talk any more than you have to. And when you do, remember, we Guatemalans say *aldea* for village, not *cantón*."

Josefina has been correcting our Salvadoran way of speaking. "It's not that our Guatemalan way is better, Felipe," she says carefully. "Your way of speaking is beautiful, too. But you don't want to draw attention to yourselves. You need to adapt, to belong everywhere. Like fish in a stream, you need to be."

"Chameleons," says Romy.

"Chameleons with language," says Josefina, smiling.

"Chameleons with tongues of silver," says Romy.

"Scarlet chameleons with tongues of silver," I add. It's a game we used to play with Jacinto.

Josefina looks at us as if making a picture in her mind. "Oh, my," she says, and sighs. "Remember, Felipe, remember, Romelia. You do have a grandmother in Hondo. Me."

AT DAWN we set off walking. The road runs east along a ridge above the river. The sun rises, dazzling, right in front of us. The land between the road and the river is steep, terraced in giant steps. From it grow peppers and lettuces, cabbages and grapes, kale, corn. Everything close together, carefully tended.

Near a wall of basalt stone, an old man dressed in white works carefully with a digging stick, loosening the soil around his plants. He sees us coming toward him, but he doesn't move away.

"Good morning, uncle," my mother greets him. "What a beautiful garden you have."

So that he won't have to answer, she speaks to us instead of to him.

"Look, *chicos*! This river, this Río Motagua, makes such rich earth."

We pause in our walking, ready to pass by if the man doesn't respond. The old man raises his head and studies us. My mother's words warn him that we are strangers. In Guatemala, just like at home, it isn't safe for peasants to be seen speaking with outsiders. So when he speaks to us, it's something, a gift.

"Here we call it Río Hondo, Deep River, and not for nothing," he says. "You don't try to swim a river like this one."

The old man must guess that we need to get across. Politely he scratches a hole in the ground with his digging stick, not looking at us. I glance at Mama. She wants to know who has a boat. How will she find out without asking?

"Is the fishing good?"

I can't help smiling. *Paloma.*

"My nephew Eusebio doesn't do too badly. Though it's been a bad season," answers the old man, without looking up.

So we know who has a boat, and that he could use money.

"Perhaps we would want to buy from him, if we knew where to find him," says my mother.

"You could inquire at the food stand, the one among banana trees just along the road, a morning's walk from here. It's run by his wife, Inés," says the uncle of Eusebio. "*Vayan con Díos,*" he adds. "Go with God."

"Stay with God," we answer politely.

HIGH NOON. We're hot and thirsty. In a daze, we almost walk right past the food stand hidden by banana leaves. Behind the counter, a tall woman stands quietly watching us, her hand on a pottery jug. She pours us water before we ask for it.

"God bless you," says Mama when she has drunk, setting down her glass with a sigh. "Would you be Inés?"

The woman nods, with just the shadow of a smile.

"We have a transportation problem." Mama looks at her feet.

Inés glances around. A boy sits behind her, peeling oranges in spirals. Inés puts her hand on his shoulder. "My son," she says. And then to Mama, "I thought you might. Do you wish to cross the river?"

Mama nods and looks over to us. "My children."

"Soldiers patrol the riverbank now," Inés says softly, sadly. "Do you have Guatemalan identification cards?"

"No."

"Those found without cards are fined a thousand *quetzales* and returned in the direction from which they came," says Inés.

"The soldiers get a reward for each refugee they turn back," the boy adds, his eyes shining. I wonder if the soldiers would reward him, if he took a notion to turn us in.

"My husband, Eusebio, will take only a hundred *quetzales* for each person to ferry you across the river in his boat," says Inés. She has blue circles under her eyes. "He doesn't do it for the money, but because he has a good heart."

"I'm sure he does," says Mama. "Love him for it," she adds. I look at her in surprise. A tear is running down her cheek, and she dashes it off with the flat of her hand.

Inés busies herself spreading cardboard behind the food stand for us to rest on.

"You'll have to cross at night," she says. "How I wish that my Eusebio were a simple fisherman again."

Romy puts her hand on my arm and whispers in my ear, "How *I* wish that Papa were just drawing pictures."

I'm surprised. What does Romy know about Jacinto's activities? What do I know, really? That they are dangerous. That they're necessary. That because Jacinto does them, they must be right.

I THINK THAT Eusebio hasn't been a simple fisherman for a long time. In the dark, his boat doesn't smell like fish. It smells like the sweat of people who are scared. I don't know if I'll be able to make myself get on it.

Other people wanting to cross the river join us in the bushes where we wait. A lot of people for such a small boat.

Because we are the smallest, Eusebio tells Romy and me to go up inside the bow.

"In there, where the anchor rope is stowed. See? Yes. Go on!"

A tiny closet. A hole where the anchor rope goes through the hull of the boat lets in a little air, but I'm thinking: if this boat turns over, we'll be trapped under there. Fear smothers me. Huddled in the closet with nothing to do, I can't make my breath go in and out.

"Felipe!" Romy pulls on my sleeve, beating my arm in the dark. I shake her off.

"Felipe, let's play!"

I shake my head no. I can't speak.

Romy puts her hands on my ears and turns my face toward her.

"Felipe," I hear her say anxiously, "if I had a cigar, I would give it to you."

I want to live. I want to breathe. I just can't.

The closet door bursts open, Romy disappears, and the next thing I know, I am slapped full in the face with a bucketful of river water. Cold water and air rush into my lungs together. I'm soaked and sputtering, and Romy is drying my head with Mama's shawl. The boat lurches away from the shore. The river is gurgling all around, but I don't think about what might happen. When Eusebio comes to let us out, we're wet, but we're okay.

EUSEBIO TALKS in a hoarse whisper that smells of tobacco, one hand on Mama's shoulder, one hand grasping my T-shirt. He's like a sheepdog, and we are the sheep. He makes us go in little groups, watching the road, listening. He stays with his passengers and sends them off into the dark a few at a time. We're the last, and he pushes us into the dark with a warm hand against my cold neck.

9

Black Boots

IN VILLAGES in Guatemala, they sell
flat white biscuits that weigh almost nothing.
Because the biscuits are light to carry, they have
become our one dependable food. We catch a
few buses: Crooked Arrow, Diesel Diablo. Most
of the time, during the day and sometimes at
night, we walk.

We find places to sleep, in the hills, under
bushes. In the early mornings, we see deer
moving in the mist, as quiet as we are.

As we get closer to the Mexican border, we
notice other groups of refugees. Many are Indians
in beautiful colorful clothes. When we meet, they
nod to us quickly, afraid to talk, their eyes on

the ground. Many are old people. Many are women carrying small children, traveling without their men.

These hills are full of women and children on the move. We remind me of prehistoric people we studied back in school, in a history book with pictures: the first settlers of Cuzcatlán. One picture is called "Foragers." The foragers are women; they carry black-eyed babies on their backs and move through forests looking for stuff to eat. They aren't smiling. Another picture, "Fighters and Hunters," is of men. They are grinning and whacking one another with bones. If I lived in prehistory, I would be too old to tag along with the foragers.

WE COME upon a creek that looks clear, and stop to drink and fill our plastic bottle. Two women step out from the bushes and greet us cautiously. Their voices have a familiar lilt.

"*Salvadoreñas?*" Paloma asks. They are. They too are headed north and tell of a river "nearby," patrolled by helicopters.

"Is there a bridge?" asks Paloma. The women murmur together, like a stream gathering strength.

"They won't let us cross the bridge. . . ."

"They capture people there, put them on trucks. . . ."

"Take them to camps where they starve."

"This is what a guide told us to do, so maybe it is what you should do, too. I don't know."

"We were told to hide in the bushes until night, then to undress and wade across the river with our clothes over our heads."

"Do you think that could be right?"

The women speak doubtfully. "Sometimes, we hear, men shoot people, from the bridge or from helicopters. . . ."

Men shoot people. I try not to think what it would be like, to be shot from above, from a helicopter.

Paloma bites her lip. She thanks the women for their warnings and advice, but when they want to join us, she shakes her head.

"You and we also will have better chances of getting across separately." They take our hands briefly, murmuring, *"Bendiga . . . bendiga,"* and then walk away.

A RAINSTORM, and it is almost night. From high on the road, Paloma sees an abandoned car, flipped off the mountain, crashed in a ravine.

We climb down to it, sliding on mud.

"I won't go in," says Romy, standing in the pouring rain, her dress plastered to her shoulder blades.

"Why not?" asks Mama.

"Because there will be the ghost of a dead person in there," says Romy.

"The person who was driving this car flew out of the window and straight to the angels," says Paloma.

"How do you know?" asks Romy, shivering.

"I looked."

LYING ON THE SEAT inside, with my feet up on the ceiling and the rain drumming against my soles, I decide to start a collection. Not things to carry around—the suitcase and the corn husks are plenty. A collection of true things to remember.

Often, back home in El Salvador, Romy went to bed before me, and I was still up when Jacinto got home. Mama and I sat at the kitchen table with Jacinto while he ate the supper we'd kept warm. Jacinto brought me cookies. I put them beside my bowl of hot coffee and dipped them in, one by one. And I watched my father Jacinto talking, worrying, laughing.

When I swung my leg under the table, I would bump his leg. Sometimes he kicked me back. Sometimes he grabbed my foot between his feet and held it.

In this wrecked car in the hills of Guatemala, listening to the rain running down the mountains and drumming on the roof, I make myself remember everything: the smell of bean soup, the clink of Jacinto's spoon. Oranges in a bowl in the middle of the table. And Jacinto, blowing on his soup, raising an eyebrow.

Jacinto doesn't shoot people.

I MUST HAVE BEEN ASLEEP. Suddenly my dream is shattered. A mean light flashes in my eyes.

"Up!" A bark like a Doberman's. "Out!"

"There's a nest of them in there," says a man's voice.

We're awake, queasy with fright, numb with tiredness. Someone is rocking the wrecked car. I see only black boots.

"Out of there, boy, before I kick you!"

I crawl out and scramble to my feet, putting distance between my face and the boots. Romy and Mama are right behind me. We stand together, holding hands.

"You're lucky we didn't shoot you," says the man, his hand on the butt of a pistol stuck in his belt.

Teenage soldiers with him nod like puppets. All three in uniform, camouflage pants. I want to dive back into my dream, my remembering.

"I suppose we'll have to take you in," says the man in charge, in a bored voice. It's dark, but my eyes are used to dark, and I can make out that he is what Jacinto might call a spit-and-polish man.

Their truck is up on the road above our hiding place. The man motions with his thumb for us to climb in the back. Paloma eyes the large cab up front. I don't know what she's planning, but I can see she is up to something. She becomes both more relaxed and more alert, like a cat. She combs out her hair with her fingers. Instead of braiding it quickly as she usually does in the morning, she shakes it back over her shoulders. Then she takes a deep breath and looks at the leader of the soldiers. Her voice sounds strange, as if perhaps she is imitating somebody in a movie.

"Oh, *Señor Capitán*, I know that I shouldn't ask this, but I am so afraid that my children are catching cold. . . ." Romy, huddled against her, gives a big sneeze. Mama puts an arm around her and takes my hand again.

"Surely you will be so kind as to let us ride up front?" Paloma actually smiles at the soldiers. I can see her teeth in the dark. I let go of Paloma's hand and wipe my hand on my pants. I see what she is up to.

"If these boys don't mind, of course," she adds, with just a trace of mockery.

The leader motions to the soldiers to ride in back.

"*Sí, sí, Capitán*," they say. "*Siempre a sus órdenes*! Just as you wish!" And they are laughing.

As we get into the cab on the passenger side, Mama pushes me in front of her, so that I have to sit next to the *capitán*. I am furious. Paloma leans across Romy and me, and looks at the *capitán*. Her eyes are like a deer's, wide but hard to see into.

"Is there a bus stop near here?" she asks, as if he were our friend. She sighs. "We are so lost." She laughs and shakes her head. "I have never before slept in a wrecked car!"

"Where were you expecting to sleep?" asks the *capitán*, fingering his mustache.

Paloma seems to be pondering this question. "I only hope not in jail," she confides at last, her voice like a cat purring. "It is not by choice that we travel, but out of necessity. *Señor Capitán* . . ."

"At your service," the man says, giving Paloma a wink.

Suddenly this short truck ride seems more dangerous than anything we have done. No! I want to say. No! No! But I am just banging my fist on my leg, my mouth shut.

"It is essential for the health and safety of my children that we cross the border to Mexico. . . ." Paloma acts lost and confused, unlike the Paloma Romy and I are used to obeying. Unlike the Mama we've always known. Unlike Jacinto's Palomitas, though a little like her. Too much like her.

Would they take the children?

Yes, love, they would. . . .

She is doing it for us. But that only makes it worse.

Paloma talks on, leaning toward the man, her hand on my knee.

"We know that we are just visitors in your country and are not needed in your jails. . . . Can you think of any way . . . ? The fine to get out of jail would be so enormous. . . ."

Paloma is offering a bribe.

The man drives awhile in silence. He lights a cigarette. He looks at Paloma from the corner of his eye. Then a smile spreads over his face. His bare teeth are ugly. One of them is gold.

MAMA'S IDENTIFICATION CARD comes in a dark blue folder. It is a little smaller than a Mexican thousand-*peso* note folded double. When you put the note inside the identification card, the edges just peep out. This is one of the things the *capitán* shows Paloma.

"An attractive little sandwich, isn't it?" he says. "Sometimes it will make a border official think that a simple identification card is a passport!"

He laughs. Paloma answers with a smile of admiration, her eyebrows raised. But when the leader pulls over for a stop, she whispers to us urgently, "Don't leave me alone with him, no matter what!"

It's your problem, I want to say. I don't, and I know it isn't.

Who would have thought the Mexican border would be so far, traveling by truck?

Paloma continues to play up to the *capitán*.

We stick to Paloma like leeches.

THE *capitán* drops off the younger soldiers and then stops at a roadside bar.

He sits down at a table with two chairs, motioning Paloma into the other seat. Romy and I quickly draw up chairs on either side of Mama. The *capitán* orders two beers. When they are brought, he gulps his down and looks sideways at me. He belches. He pulls some *quetzales* out of his pocket.

"Take your sister and buy her a Popsicle."

I feel my ears burning red. The things I think, I can't say.

"I don't like Popsicles, thank you," Romy says loudly, fiercely. She is learning to fake like Paloma. But she is making her lie true. She will probably never eat a Popsicle again. Mama's eyebrows shoot up, and she has pink spots on her cheeks.

Romy stares at the *capitán*. He stares back. Under his khaki collar, his neck is getting as red as a turkey buzzard's.

Paloma clears her throat. "*Señor Capitán*," she says. "Perhaps we have a slight misunderstanding. We need help, yes, and transportation. But we are quite willing to pay. In money." She takes her *quetzales* from her pouch and carefully gives half of the roll of bills to the *capitán*. "We are grateful—" Her tone has become formal. The *capitán* doesn't let her finish.

"*Hija de puta!*" In one quick movement he grabs the other half of the bills, slaps Paloma hard across the face, and stands up, knocking over his chair, grabbing Romy and me by our shirts. He throws us into the truck, and Paloma jumps in beside us. The *capitán* drives us at breakneck speed through a small town that I realize is on the Mexican border only because we cross a concrete bridge with soldiers on it. The *capitán* doesn't even slow down.

He screeches to a halt outside of town, and while we hurry to get out, he is pushing us, looking over his shoulder. He takes off so fast, he leaves a smell of burned rubber.

"Thank God," says Paloma, as his truck disappears into traffic.

"*Mamí*," Romy says, speaking for us both, "never do that again."

"You are right," says Paloma, almost her old self again. "I would far rather walk."

"Seventy kilometers?" I ask.

"Any number of kilometers," says Mama.

I can see she needs cheering up.

"Think of all the money we won't have to lug around," I say.

10

The Letter

"HOW MANY more countries, Baba?"
Romy asks tiredly. She does have a cold. We are
camped in a dark corner of the bus station in
Mexico City. Romy sits on a red plastic chair,
wrapped in Mama's shawl. Her legs, sticking
out, are muscled like a soccer player's, but the
rest of her is looking small.

"Half of Mexico, and the United States," says
Mama. "Then we'll be in Canada."

"Mexico and the U.S. are big suckers, though.
Grandotes," I say. "Ten times bigger than
Guatemala."

Romy crosses her eyes and rolls them back in
her head.

"Stop that!" Mama says automatically. "They'll stick that way."

I look at my sneakers, stuck out on the floor in front of me. The rubber is flapping off the ends. "If it were hopscotch, we'd be on square four."

"Quiet, *chicos*," says Paloma, whispering. "Some Mexicans are getting fed up with refugees. So don't let on. They don't want us, even just passing through."

Romy's eyes roll up again. Mama threatens her with the side of her hand. Romy starts to hum. She doesn't want to hear this conversation, and I don't want to have it.

"What would they do?" I ask, as if I couldn't guess by now.

"Question us and make us prove we are Mexican."

We sit in silence, all three too tired to think up a story.

Romy dozes off. Her head flops to one side, and she begins to snore.

"Okay," says Paloma, taking a deep breath to shake off her own sleepiness. "Let's get started: where shall we be from, Felipe?"

"I don't know. Chiapas?" Chiapas is in the south of Mexico.

Mama wrinkles her nose. "Chiapas has lots of refugees living there. They probably don't even want people from Chiapas. . . . But I think some Chiapans are Indians. They look like us, and they talk more like us than the people up here do."

She sits thinking, staring into space, and suddenly her eyes light on a metal ashtray spilling over with trash. In it are several crumpled envelopes. She goes and gets them, brings them back to where we are, smooths them out.

"Heh!" she says, picking one up and looking hard at the postmark. She gets up again and goes to a big tourist map on one wall of the station. I am mystified enough to stagger to my feet and follow her.

"There it is. Monterrey!" She points to a city in the northern part of Mexico.

"Monterrey is where we're from now?"

"It's not where we're from, but it's where we're going!"

I take the envelope from her and look inside. Tickets, maybe? Nothing.

"Wait with Romy," Paloma orders, and goes off to a magazine stand.

She comes back with two sheets of stationery. "Your pen."

When I give it to her, she sits with the end between her teeth and looks at me out of the corner of her eye. I don't know what she is thinking.

"You're going to have to help me with this," she says at last. "Here's the idea. We are from Chiapas, where there has been much trouble. Your papa has gone to Monterrey to find work in construction. In a city of that size they will be building—what?"

"Hotels."

"Yes. He has gone to work on the construction of a hotel. But oh! He misses his family. So he writes to them. Dear wife, he says, dear children. I long to see you. Please take this money and get yourselves tickets and come to join me. . . ."

"I have found a beautiful house . . . ," I suggest.

"An apartment," interrupts Paloma, "small but clean, with big windows."

As I think what to say next, Jacinto's face hovers in my mind. He is looking down at the soup in his spoon, blowing on it, thinking.

"And there is a school nearby . . ."

"that the neighbors say is strict and well directed . . ."

"and has an excellent soccer team."

"Felipe will be glad to hear this," completes Mama.

"Your lonely and devoted father . . . Ja—," I say. Mama looks at me quickly, and I shut my mouth.

"Your lonely and devoted father, Eusebio Ramón. . . . Come on, Felipe, we need a surname."

I swallow a lump in my throat. "What's the name on the envelope?"

Paloma grabs my shoulder. "Felipe! Of course. How could I have forgotten? The envelope!"

We both look at the envelope. *Señor* M. A. Cortez, it says.

"Yes, yes," she says, bouncing in her chair. "Eusebio Ramón Cortez. Bless his heart. And I will be M. A. . . . María Alvarez Cortez!"

For no reason I think of Paloma and Jacinto working together at the kitchen table at home, Jacinto writing, Mama checking things on a list, carefully printing addresses.

I put our suitcase across my knees and lean the paper on it. Carefully, I write everything Paloma said. I sign the letter with a flourish and hand it to her. She folds it carefully and slips it into the envelope. Then she takes the pen and adds an *a* to the address, changing *Señor* to *Señora*.

She breathes a sigh of satisfaction.

"Postmarked from Monterrey just one week ago. . . . Now, go to sleep," Paloma orders. I do, dreaming my way into the letter, dreaming it true.

SHOUTS, CALLS, loudspeakers, diesel fumes. Bus stations are loud and full of smells. And crowded. Plus, you don't want to put your suitcase down because somebody might think it's his. You want to rest your eyes and your ears, but you can't. I catch sight of the three of us in a mirror that makes up part of a wall. I notice that my eyebrows are getting very black and fierce.

We go from one station to another, changing buses, making our way north in a zigzag. Twice Paloma tells our story to Mexican authorities, tells of Eusebio Ramón waiting for us, tells of the troubles in Chiapas and the good prospects in Monterrey. She shows the letter to back up her story. Twice with no problem. Proudly I wiggle my eyebrows at Romy.

The third time, a Mexican immigration official, a *migra*, wakes us up in the middle of the night. The bus is stopped. Paloma carries her pouch around her waist now, but she fumbles for it automatically, feeling for the string around her neck. She's still asleep and doesn't have her wits about her.

"We're going to Monterrey," I tell the man.

"Yes? And from where?"

"Yaxha, in Chiapas."

"What is the capital of the state of Chiapas?" asks the *migra* official.

I feel a tremble go through Mama.

"Uhhh . . . ," she begins.

My throat is dry. I can't think of a thing to say.

"My brother is going to play soccer," Romy announces suddenly, in a high, braggy voice. "He's really good, and Papa says the Monterrey professional team is the best, and some of the high schools have stupendous teams. And there's one kid from Monterrey who is so fast that the Russians are trying to get him to be on their team—who was it?"

I can't believe it. Where has she gotten all this?

"Flores? Torres?" says the *migra*, searching his mind.

"Emilio Flores!" says a man behind us.

The *migra* slaps his forehead. "Of course!" And he moves on back, talking soccer and absent-mindedly checking the identification papers of the people behind us.

Behind his back, Romy gives me a look of pure joy.

OUR BUS STRAINS over mountains, lurches around curves, hurtles through darkness, creeps across desert. Mostly I sleep. Once I wake to see a boy standing on the edge of the road, dangling a rattlesnake on a stick. Another time Romy wakes me because she sees a cactus and thinks it is a bear dancing in the desert.

In my sleep I dream of Jacinto, my real father, whose name is not Eusebio Ramón Cortez, but Jacinto Ramirez.

He's walking down the street in Canada. I know it's Canada because the buildings are tall and clean. Jacinto is laughing with happiness. In one hand he has an orange, and he pitches it to me like a baseball.

11

Coyote

"WILL WE EVER see green trees again?" I ask Mama. Four days we have been on this bus out of Mexico City. "Purple mountains? Yellow cornfields?" Abuela, Chuy.

Paloma looks past me, out of the bus window. "What's the matter, *chico*? You don't like earth colors? You don't like dust?"

I think of Abuela, with her hands muddy from planting ocotillos. Sure, I like earth colors. Maybe this landscape just needs a little water.

Romelia, peering through the window, sees a road sign. "*Mamí! Estados Unidos*, fifty kilometers! It's nothing, fifty kilometers. We could walk it in a day!"

"Shhh!" whispers Paloma. "Who says we are going to the United States?"

Romy pops her hand over her mouth, but her eyes are shining. Later, when Mama is dozing, she whispers to me:

"Just the United States now, and then Canada, right?"

"Right."

"Will he be there?"

Jacinto.

I shrug and feel tears sting suddenly behind my eyelids. We both look at Mama. Would she drag us so far if she didn't hope he'd be there?

DESERT. SHACKS. Dusty gardens. Clotheslines. Trash dumps. We reach a border city in the north of Mexico, and stumble off the bus into a loud, crowded square by a river. The Río Bravo. The Grande. Speakers set up in the square are playing a *ranchera*, music we know from home, a song Rafa used to play on his guitar. The wind catches in the speakers and makes them wail.

I get off the bus before Mama, and then turn to watch her and Romy step down into the neon light of the street lamp. Mama's face shines yellow in the harsh light: she looks tired and lonely. Maybe she wants to turn around. To go back home. She catches me looking at her and smiles. "I have a surprise for you, *chicos*!" she says. "Our very first hotel."

OUR OWN ROOM! Luxury. Delight. Our room, with pink walls and a lock on the door that we can turn ourselves. A heavy metal key, stamped with number 14. And a bathroom with a shower. Hot and cold water. Soap in a paper. In and out of the shower we go, again and again. There are clean sheets on the bed, stiff with starch. We lie flat, clean and wet, and tell stupid jokes. Paloma starts a pillow fight. I knock over the lamp, and somebody in the next room bangs on the wall.

I think the best smell in the world might be clean sheets and soap.

In our clean beds, we sleep right through the night until early morning. Wake up starving.

"Let's go out and take a look at this town," says Paloma.

The way she speaks, so calmly, you would never guess what a day this is. All borders are tough. But the Mexico-U.S. border is famous for being the toughest. Paloma acts as easy as if we were going on a picnic.

"Can we leave our things?" Stupid bags. Mama looks at the old suitcase Beatriz gave her. She folds the clothes in it and smooths them, even though they are dirty. She closes the suitcase gently. She puts the packet with the letter from Father Gustavo around her neck. She leaves the suitcase on the bed.

"Will we go to the United States today?" Romy asks, jumping on the bed like a circus performer about to make a great leap. "It's just across the river!" *The Flying Ramirez Family*.

"Not today," Paloma says.

Romy flops down on the bed, disappointed. She pulls the pillow over her face.

Paloma looks at me and draws a breath, wearily preparing to give an explanation.

"Romy," I say, "we can't just walk across the bridge. You need papers to do that: papers or money. Even if our money is enough for a bribe, Mama has to figure out who to give it to."

"I know," Romy mumbles from under the pillow. "Are we going uphill all the time, Felipe?"

"No. It only looks like that on the map."

Romy lies still. "Sure," she says after a while. Mama is brushing her hair. She catches my eye in the mirror and smiles. There are gold flecks in her eyes.

"But think of this," I tell Romy. "We can take a stroll in the morning coolness. No suitcase. No sack to lug. We can have coffee, and food. We can pretend we live here."

IN THE SQUARE in front of the hotel, old men are out early to greet the day.

People are selling food. Smells float to meet us, so good that I feel faint. I see Romy open her mouth, and before she can plead or say a word, Paloma holds out a red *peso* bill to a taco maker, to pay for a meat and egg *taquito*. We eat it, and Romy licks the juice that runs down her hand. We buy another one and divide it, too. Paloma puts the change in her pocket and rattles it like a rich gringo, raising her eyebrows to make us laugh.

We wander toward the bridge, greeting the street vendors who are just setting up. Many people are crossing the bridge in both directions. It looks easy.

Of course there is a guardhouse on the bridge, with police in front. The people waiting in line are pulling out their papers. I glance at Paloma, but she and Romy are leaning over the bridge parapet on their stomachs, watching the second-hand vendors spreading out clothes on big trestle tables. Romy and Mama talk and point.

"Ooooh! A pink halter top!"

"Romy! Do you want to look like Minnie Mouse?"

Mama likes Romy to wear little white blouses that button right up to the neck.

We find some steps and go on down below the bridge. Paloma works her way along the tables, turning things and looking at them carefully. She holds a shirt against me and makes a face. She looks at the tags to see where things were made. Like buying clothes at home.

"I only want shorts," I say. "It's too hot here for anything else."

"A son of mine will wear a shirt, even among the gringos."

Romy has her hand on a plush pig, stroking its softness.

"Do you like him?" Mama asks.

Romy just smiles.

"Shall we get him?" asks Mama, and I think she wants to. I wonder if Paloma herded pigs when she was little.

Romy nods. Mama picks up the pig and signals to the vendor.

"And you, Felipe, is there one you want?"

I look at the stuffed animals: rabbits of many colors, plastic dolls with loosely rolling eyes, bears, dogs. I want Payaso. I shake my head.

Paloma hands the vendor a few coins for the pig.

"Let's call him Cipitio," says Romy.

"You know about the Cipitio?" Mama asks, surprised.

"Of course! The one who plays in ashes!"

After that, Paloma buys us shorts, in very bright, gringo-style prints, and T-shirts with Made in the U.S.A. tags. We walk down by the river, and when we come to a beach park, she and Romy slip behind some bushes and change.

"You, Felipe, keep on your old pants for swimming," says Paloma. "Roll them up."

Don't lose your pants, boy! But the money is almost gone.

WE WADE in the cool water. The other side of the river is not so very far away, maybe one hundred meters, but the water in the middle flows rapidly. It looks deep out there. I splash Romy and we chase each other. Every now and then I look at Paloma to guess what plan she is making. Impossible to tell: she just sits in the shade in her gringo shorts, building a little mound of sand over her foot.

"Psst!"

Romy and I look toward the bushes. A man is there, so still I don't see him at first: a thin brown man in a swimsuit, dark glasses, and a shirt that shows off his muscles.

"Psst! You!" he says again. I wade a little closer, but not within reach. He whispers to me in Spanish, the kind they speak in Mexico.

"Where are you from, kid?"

I point vaguely up the river.

He smiles, showing missing teeth.

"Sure," he says. "Where is it? Guatemala? El Salvador? Trying to get into the States?"

I shrug my shoulders as if I don't know what he is talking about. Romy stands knee-deep in water, staring from him to me. From where Paloma sits, she can't see the man, but she can see us. She gets up and comes over casually. When she sees the man, she calls to us in the clear voice she uses for fooling people:

"Go, play while you have a chance to get cool, because we need to be going home soon."

We splash and wade, not too far from Paloma. She and the man argue in low voices. I hear numbers mentioned, money. My heart starts beating fast. This is a *coyote*, then, one of the men who make their living smuggling people like us across the border.

Finally Paloma calls us over. She parts the bushes, and there, lying on the bank spotted with sun, is a big black inner tube from a truck tire. On one side the man is tying a rope. On the other end of the rope is a harness. The man takes it in his hand and wades into the water. The tube follows him, bobbing along. Mama goes and gets our old clothes, my new shorts, and Cipitio. She gives the *coyote* some money. She puts the clothes into a plastic bread bag the vendor gave her. It makes a little packet, which she swings in a loop.

"All aboard," she says cheerfully. "Uncle is going to give us a ride."

Romy laughs.

I glance at "Uncle." He appears to be all business. He bites his lower lip and keeps a flickering eye on the riverbank. No one else is in sight.

"Wait!" says Paloma. "We must all sit down at once."

We step into the middle of the tube, and all together, we sit. The balance is pretty good. We hang on to one another, weaving a circle with our arms.

The *coyote* steps into deeper water. Looking quickly up and down the river, he slips the harness over his shoulders. He starts swimming, a quick, strong breaststroke, and we bob across behind him. Romy holds Cipitio between her knees.

THE OTHER SIDE is quiet. Dirty gray sand and dark bushes. Romy and I look hard at the bushes. They are dusty and still. No black boots. A big smile spreads over Romy's face.

We step free of the tube. Romy wrings out Cipitio and then, holding him under her arm, tries to wring out her shirttails. The *coyote* holds out his hand as if expecting something from Paloma. . . . The *coyote* holds out his hand. Paloma shakes her head. The *coyote* stops smiling, grabs Mama's arm, and pulls it behind her back. Mama yelps with pain. I pick up a stick, ready to hit the *coyote*, but Mama gives me the smallest shake of her head.

Paloma is playacting! She is crying without tears. When she's really hurt, really scared, she doesn't yelp or curse: she cries like a squirt gun.

Romy and I watch, amazed. Cursing and struggling, Paloma empties the plastic bag onto the sand with her free hand. The clothes fall out, and the hotel key jingles. The *coyote* kicks at our things, holding on to Paloma as he searches with his foot.

"Ouch! Take it, then," she says in a voice full of fake despair. "There *is* more money—in the room. There's a false bottom—ouch!—in the suit-case. It was—for my sister!"

The *coyote* looks at Paloma. He doesn't know that she is fooling him. I hold tight to my stick and stare at the *coyote*. I want to hit somebody, and not just him. We are the ones who are lying now. The *coyote* expected more. She paid him only half.

He finally lets go of Mama.

"Change your clothes here, before you go up on the highway," says the *coyote*. "Otherwise, people will call you a wetback; they will know you just came across the river." I wish he wouldn't be kind. He puts the key in his pocket. Number 14.

"*Vayan,*" he says. "Go," and he wades back into the water.

"With God, does he mean, or to hell?" Romy asks Mama, her face serious, curious. Are we turning into bad guys? Mama shrugs. We don't know what he meant. Though I know what he'll say when he finds that old suitcase.

12

Teeth

THE *coyote* paddles slowly back across the river, dragging his tube. I watch him out of sight, my jaws aching. My top teeth are still clamped behind the lower ones. I feel sorry for the *coyote*, sorry we cheated him. And as if I left all my cat's luck on the other side of the river.

"Whoa!" Paloma shakes herself. "Well, let's go." We cautiously stick our heads out of the bushes that grow along the river. We look up and down. We don't see anybody, so we climb the embankment to the hot, black highway. "East," Paloma decides.

We walk east on the melting tarmac. Bits of gravel stick to our shoes. The sun slowly sinks, and our shadows creep out ahead of us. Romy and I make a game of trying to step on our shadows' heads.

"What are we going to do when it gets dark, Mama?" Romy asks.

Paloma doesn't answer right away. How could she? She must be tired of trying to sound as if she knows when she doesn't. I try to picture the map and the border we just crossed. The Río Grande, gurgling brownly between Mexico and Texas, U.S.A.

Río Hondo, Río Chixoy, Río de la Pasión, Río Salsipuedes, Río Grande . . .

On the map, we are just halfway. A handspan from El Salvador. A handspan from Canada.

And so busy making our money stretch that we are turning into cheaters.

Romy comes up behind me, throwing a black shadow just to my left. I jump out, land on her shadow's head, and hear a loud screech. Mama screams: a beat-up pickup truck slams on brakes just behind us, and a man sticks his face out.

"Chicos!" he shouts, thinking we were all kids, ready to yell at us. Then he takes a second look at

Paloma. She gives him a little nod, without smiling. He lifts his straw hat in a gesture of greeting and smiles broadly. He wears a gold cross dangling in the opening of his shirt.

"You'll be wanting to find the camp for *mojados*?" he asks in Spanish. Wetbacks, he calls us. Like the *coyote* said.

"Yes," says Paloma. "We are going there to greet friends." Another lie, to show we aren't alone. Our clothes are still damp with the water of the river.

The man jerks his head toward the seat next to him. He reaches over to open the door. We look at one another, and then we all pile in, me first, closest to the man. Empty beer cans crunch under our feet. Dice made of felt swing from the mirror. "Your friends are coming from . . .?"

"El Salvador," Romy says, before Mama can kick her foot to keep her quiet. Poor Romy. Tell a lie, and you worry about going to hell. Tell the truth; you get your foot stomped.

We ride on in silence. No one is legally allowed to enter the United States from El Salvador.

We come to a tin road sign. The man slows and points to it, spelling out the words: TRANSIENT SHELTER.

"This is the place you're looking for." We take his word for it.

He swerves the truck off the black road onto a dirt path, then drives through bushes again until we come to a big shed. The shed has a concrete floor and a tin roof. You can tell from the smell that somebody peed on the floor. Paloma's mouth twists down in disgust. She likes things clean. She looks at the man who brought us here, and her eyes fall on the cardboard boxes in the back of his truck.

"I beg a favor," she says formally, the first words she has spoken to him since we got into the truck. He grins and makes a little bow.

"At your service . . ."

My heart sinks.

She doesn't return the smile.

"May we have a box?" she asks.

"You may have anything I can give you, *señora.*"

He looks very happy, takes the boxes from the back, asks my mother where she wants them. Still she doesn't smile at him. I see a tree with well-spaced low branches and nudge Romy:

"Look! A watchtower!" We take off running. Romy is good at trees. She grins and stuffs Cipitio in her shirt. She reaches the tree before

I do, grabs a branch, and scrambles up like a monkey. Up and up we go. Romy is laughing, and every time she slows down, I give her a boost with my head. We are high up in the pink sky when I think I hear a scream. Maybe some animal. Then we hear Paloma calling shrilly.

We both groan when we hear her voice. We want to climb forever.

"*Chicos!* Come down right now. We need to get things ready for our friends. Ramón and Eusebio will be here at any moment!"

If only.

It's nearly dusk, and the crickets are singing so loudly in the trees that we can hardly hear her. When we get down from the tree, there's a struggle going on. The man is holding Paloma's shoulder; she is pushing him away. Romy and I close in, one on each side of Paloma, and the man lets go.

Mama looks confused, totally flustered. She rips off three flaps from one of the boxes and gives us each one. We begin sweeping off a part of the concrete floor. Mama is shaking. She sweeps the concrete so hard, the cardboard shreds. Piles of dead crickets line the walls, and they give off a sweet, sick smell. We dump them on the ground outside.

"Do we *have* to sleep here?" Romelia asks. The man with the pickup truck hangs around, smiling. In the stillness of the evening, the only sound is more crickets.

"We will wait for Eusebio," my mother says, her voice higher than usual. "He will be here soon."

To the man she says, "Please go away now. We do not wish for you to wait."

Very slowly, the man gets in his truck.

"See you later!" he calls as he drives off.

I hope not.

WE ALL SLEEP in a heap on one piece of cardboard. In the middle of the night Mama tickles us awake. The moon is full. Mama is talking nervously.

"I'm sorry," she says. "I feel so stupid."

"What is it, Mama?"

"I'm afraid to go pee by myself!"

"We'll come with you."

"But there's no outhouse."

"No," says Mama. "There are the woods. And thank you for coming with me."

So we get up and stumble a little way into the bushes. Romelia and I turn our backs to Mama and try to keep ourselves awake.

We hear the sound of a motor. We know before we see it that the pickup truck is coming back. Mama grabs us and pulls us farther into the woods. We stay very still and we don't peek out, but we hear the man's voice and then the voice of another man. They are drunk, and they are quarreling. They talk in a mix of Spanish and English, and use lots of swearwords. I understand only a little.

"What the . . . ? A stuffed pig!"

I see Cipitio sail through the air.

"You didn't say anything about kids!"

". . . lock them in the truck."

"So where is she?"

There is a crash. The tinkling of a bottle breaking on concrete. More bad words.

Truck doors slamming.

Motor gunning.

Tires screeching. Gears grinding.

Don't hit a tree, I pray. Don't have a flat. Just keep going.

By the time the sounds of the truck fade away, Romy is asleep on the ground.

I stay with Romy while Paloma gets our things, and we begin walking again. The tar of the road is still warm, and the bullfrogs are croaking. Mama has her arm over my shoulder, and I let her, because Mama seems to me now like a wounded soldier. Romelia holds her hand. Under Romy's arm is Cipitio, the flying pig.

For a long time Paloma shakes. But no cars or trucks come by, and after a while the sun rises.

I WORRY ABOUT PALOMA, and I guess Romy does, too.

We are passing by a store. Though it's still only September, the store window has a display of things for the Day of the Dead, which is at the end of October: masks, skulls, costumes. I'm looking at these things, and suddenly Romy jumps.

"Mamí!" she says. "Could I please, please, have just a few American *centavos*, and Felipe, too?"

By miracle, Paloma, who worries all the time about money, says yes without even asking why, and she goes with us into the store. Romelia heads straight to the costume part, where she finds a card of black stickers. On the card is the picture of a pirate smiling, showing black gaps where some of his teeth should be. Romy frowns at the number on the price tag, counts her money, and pays the salesgirl without saying a word in English or Spanish. Mama is as impressed as I am. She looks at me, raises her eyebrows, widens her eyes. She smiles as Romy comes back to us.

"For you, Mama!" Romy says.

Paloma looks at the card a minute and then ducks into a changing booth. When she comes out, she gives us a big, ugly grin that would scare off Dracula himself. It appears that three of her front teeth have been knocked out.

It's a shock. Before we can say a word, Paloma goes over to the place where they sell sewing supplies. She finds some scissors attached to a cardboard with white elastic. She takes these back into the changing room. When she reappears, I don't recognize her. For a split second it seems that the store mirror has come to life. Paloma has chopped off all her beautiful hair, cut it as short as a boy's. She looks like me, but with bad teeth. Romy covers her eyes. Paloma, standing like a kid in her gringo shorts, works the scissors back onto the cardboard and hangs them on the display rack.

13

Abuelita

A CHINESE RESTAURANT. We go in,
wanting soup for breakfast. The waiter eyes us
suspiciously. Paloma looks like a thug. The soup
makes the patches fall off her teeth. Mama spits
them out delicately, putting them beside her
bowl like fish bones. The waiter laughs and
gives us each a fortune cookie. He translates
mine for me. It says, YOUR DETERMINATION
WILL CARRY YOU FAR.

"*Por supuesto*," says Paloma. "Very perceptive."

Romy's says, LOOK FOR GOOD TIMES
AHEAD.

Paloma's says, THE COMPANY OF FRIENDS
IS THE TONIC AT THE END OF A DAY'S

WORK. Mama frowns while the waiter explains this. Then she points suddenly out the window. "Look, Romy! A little bird!" While Romy is looking out the window, Paloma quickly trades her fortune for Romy's.

We lock ourselves in the rest room and count our money. Mama takes a bunch of the U.S. dollars out of my waistband. The waiter gives us directions to the bus station. After buying tickets, we have change. Since Paloma thinks it will be a long ride, we buy more food for the trip.

What a good feeling to be on the bus, headed away from the Río Grande, rolling through Texas, U.S.A. To sit down, to swing our feet and let the bus do the work.

Your determination will carry you far.

"Felipe, put this chicken under the seat."

Paloma hands me a red-and-white-striped box. It gives me a start when I see her hair.

"Prop the lemonade against the side of the bus so it won't tip over and leak out."

We are settled; I can look out again. The windows are dusty, but the road is even. On both sides, brown almost-desert goes as far as I can see. There are small, dusty trees in patches like the fur on a mangy dog.

I see nothing rich about the United States. The road is smoother, and some of the cars that pass us are pretty fancy. Except for that, it looks just like Mexico.

In the distance the warm wind is kicking up sand twisters.

"Your abuela Ana thinks that the devil is present in those little whirlwinds," says Mama from the seat behind us. An older woman greets us in Spanish and settles beside Mama. She is wide and has a big shopping bag on her knees, so there is no room for us.

I watch the sand twisters dancing over the dried-up ground, two of them, round and round like dogs playing.

"The devil is present only in people," Romy announces.

I punch her. She makes me nervous with her sudden wisdom. And what people does she mean, anyway? Romy punches me back. I know where she's ticklish. Soon I have her begging for mercy.

Paloma and the woman beside her rise as one. They grab us from behind and pull us apart.

"*Chicos!*" Paloma scolds. "Grow up!"

We turn on our knees so we can talk to them over the back of the seat.

"Here in Texas they call them dust devils," the woman says. "My little granddaughter used to cry when she saw them, so I started calling them *angelitos*, and now she claps her hands....You going far?"

Mama makes a vague gesture toward the road ahead.

"I crossed over fifteen years ago from Mexico," the woman says. Her face breaks into many wrinkles as she smiles. "When I arrived, I got work picking oranges. Making money! I couldn't believe it. I bought a little trailer house. I was so happy; I wrote postcards to my family. 'Wish you were here,' I said. So everybody crossed over: my brother and all his kids, my old father. . . . I let them have the trailer, and I moved out into the yard and set up a little tent. I tell them: my house is your house, but my tent is my own."

Paloma has on her friendly face, but she isn't talking. I have questions I want to ask, but from my mother's face I think it isn't yet time to ask them. The woman doesn't care if we ask or not. She is a spout of information.

"And up ahead there's another border crossing, you know."

Paloma jumps. Color rushes to her cheeks, making her face look more pointy than ever. "But we are inside the U.S. border!"

"Yes, but they check the papers again at a guardhouse this side of Harlingen."

My mother blows her breath out suddenly, so that her hair in front stands straight up for a second.

"Cheaters."

The old woman takes her hand and pats it. "Wait just a minute," she says. She puts her shopping bag on Paloma's knees. She hauls herself out of the seat, and holding the back of each seat, she makes her way to the front of the bus. She sits down behind the driver and taps him. We see that he is talking with her over his shoulder, but we can't hear what they are saying.

The woman comes back to us, nodding her head. She takes my mother's hand again. "Before the immigration guardhouse, there is a big bend in the road. If you like, the bus driver will let you out there. If you take the path through the woods, going straight north, you will reach the road again on the other side of the guardhouse. From there you should be able to get a ride into the town of Harlingen."

Paloma pulls out her ticket, a carbon copy of the one the bus driver tore off as we got on the bus. "And in Harlingen will I have to buy another bus ticket to Houston? Forty-seven more dollars?"

The woman sighs. "*Chica*, I didn't think of everything." She rises heavily, shaking her head. "You are just like me," she says to Paloma. She goes back up and talks to the driver. We can see him shrugging his shoulders, gesturing with his free hand. Finally, his eyes still glued to the road, he reaches for his big leather pouch. The woman comes back with our tickets in her hand.

"Tell the people in Harlingen that you got a ride with relatives after you bought the tickets. They are used to all this foolishness."

My mother smiles at the woman at last. She says, "*Abuelita*, Grandmother. Thank you for everything."

The woman is embarrassed by her thanks and smooths Romelia's hair.

"CAN YOU TELL US anything about the path we are to take? The path through the woods," Paloma asks.

"Well, I hear that it is not very much of a path, and that it takes a good part of the day. It is maybe ten miles long, sixteen kilometers, more or less."

I feel that the people around us have stopped their own conversations and are listening to ours. A head pops up from the seat in front of us. A young woman, with orange hair around a friendly brown face.

"I just had to butt in," she says. "I'm Linda. I have a friend who came through that way. He said those woods are crawling with rattlesnakes."

I feel Romy stiffen next to me.

"You got any socks?"

"Excuse me?" says Paloma.

"Socks," says Linda. "You're going to need some good heavy socks so they won't strike you on the ankles."

"The snakes?" my mother asks faintly. None of us has socks.

"Wait a minute," says Linda, bending down to rummage in her bag. She sits back up with a package of twelve pairs of socks, white, the kind basketball players wear. She's been to the big markets, too.

"Here," she says. "Just take them. I got plenty. Put on all of them."

"The *migra* put snakes in those woods just to keep wetbacks out," I hear a voice explaining to someone behind us.

"There are enough rattlesnakes in Texas that nobody needs to put them there," says our *abuelita*. "You know what they sound like, son?"

I stick my finger in the air like the rattle on a snake tail and make the sound between my teeth. *Abuelita* nods.

"So listen out," she says, "and don't sit down on rocks. That's where they hide."

THE BUS SLOWS to a stop. The driver glances in his rearview mirror, then motions us out. Paloma puts her hand on the driver's for a moment, in thanks, as we pass him. We climb down onto the road. The bus door gives a sigh and closes. Through the dirty window I see Linda crossing herself.

We look at one another, standing there on the deserted road. We each have legs made fat by four layers of sport socks, which are big enough to pull up past our knees, over the legs of our pants. Mama holds open the empty sock bag and collects our shoes.

There we stand, like old-fashioned shepherds. I'm carrying the chicken in the box with the red and white stripes. Romy has the lemonade and Cipitio. Paloma has the two plastic bags.

Paloma takes a deep breath.

"Follow me to the picnic!" she says, swinging the bags over her shoulder. "This *chica* is heading north."

She sets off straight down the path into the short, dusty trees, with Romy and me close behind.

14

San Jorge and the Snail

ROMY HAS A HORROR of snakes. It started a few years ago, when she was five.

Jacinto was away someplace, Guatemala, I think. We were out of money and staying at Abuela's. Mama's friend Rosario, who works on a coffee plantation, invited Mama to help with the harvest there. The coffee bosses don't pay children to work, but they will feed you tortillas and salt if you are over eight and have worked steadily. So Paloma and Rosario took me and Rosario's daughter Pina so that we would be fed, and Romy came along to be with us.

We had two jobs. One was to pull out the weeds near the coffee plants. The other was to crawl around and pick up the beans that fell on the ground, the ones taller people might miss.

We were careful about snakes, and Mama always carried a stick and kept it nearby. One day Pina wandered off, looking for beans. Romy went to find her, to put her beans in Pina's basket. Suddenly, we all heard a cry from Romy and then more cries, like a little dog barking. We all ran to where she was. We found Pina dead. Romy was still hitting the snake with a branch, again and again.

AS ROMY GOES into these woods in Texas, her face is like a mask carved of olive wood, with beads of sweat around the eyes and a whiteness around the mouth. I don't want to carry her, so I think fast.

"Romy, let's pretend. You and I will be *caballeros*, knights of old, San Jorge and San Miguel. The snakes will be the dragons."

I pick up a stick for each of us.

"This is your lance—here! Put Cipitio in your shirt. Now . . ."

Crouched and ready, we creep forward, turning to cover our backs, holding the sticks before us. Color starts coming back to Romy's face. Hot wind blows, moving the mesquite trees. Hot sun shines through their dusty leaves, making dancing shadows on the rocks. Under the rocks are strips of shade where snakes live.

"Beware," I tell Romy, trying to talk the way people do in books. "A dragon's lair lies ahead under yonder rock." We wave our sticks and sidle past.

I step over a root on the path. It comes to life and wriggles into the bushes. "Forward!" I yell, before Romy notices. We hurry to catch up with Paloma. *"Adelante!"* We slash our way past her. "Take this," I cry, and throw her the box of chicken. "Alas, not a serpent in sight! Come, trusty companion." I drag Romy forward. Paloma stands watching with her mouth open. She doesn't read books much.

IT'S NOON because the sun is straight above us. The smell of chicken is making us hungry.

There is no place where we feel safe sitting down. In the bright sun, there are scorpions the same color as the dust, their little tails curled back, ready to sting. The wind whirls sounds around—the drone of insects, the rustling of dry leaves, the scurryings of small animals we don't see. From far away, we can sometimes hear trucks passing on the highway. A hawk flies over, very quiet, his shadow passing like a ghost bird on the ground. Then we hear a sudden squeak as a mouse or other little animal is grabbed away into the sky. Beyond all these sounds, we listen for the rattle of snakes.

We eat standing up, walking, tossing the chicken bones into bushes, poking the empty box quickly under a rock. It is good to be rid of it. We drink down the warm lemonade and leave the carton. I think of the watercooler at home, damp and cold, filled every day from the tap on the street. If I was home, I would push open the door to my own house, fall on the floor of the entry, where it is cool, and rest.

AFTERNOON CLOUDS are building up in the west. We are still walking, and glad of the coolness. Soon the sky is black. You can see forks of lightning stabbing down through the bank of thunderheads. There is a free, crazy feeling in the air. Romy starts to spin around and around. A brown mouse darts across my foot. Romy sings at the top of her lungs about a snail:

"This is not the moon,
This is not the sun,
This is a snail shell,
Turn, turn, turn!"

Paloma and I join her. We are all yelling, spinning around. A crash of thunder makes Romy jump and hug Mama.

"It's only *thunder*!" Paloma exclaims. "Romy! It's not guns!"

I turn my face up to feel the first big drops of rain.

We are soaking wet when we see the highway. Mama pulls our clothes out from our bodies, trying to dry them enough so that they won't stick to us. She smooths our hair back out of our eyes. She shakes water out of her ears and tries to fluff up her own short hair. We peel off the socks and wring them out. We put all the socks in the plastic bag and put on our own shoes. How do we look?

"Clean, anyway," says Paloma.

WE STAND BEHIND a bush, watching for cars.

The first headlights are close together, like those on a jeep. We stay behind the bush. The next headlights are far apart, like those on an old car. Paloma steps out and we step out, too, one on each side of her. The car slows and pulls over to the side of the road.

It is a long, fancy car called Cadillac, such as only generals ride in in El Salvador. The window on the passenger side slides down automatically. A blast of cold air comes from inside the car. Cold air and cigar smoke. A man in a business suit looks out, his face red from leaning over.

"Harlingen?" asks my mother, pointing up the road to the north.

"Ugointa Harlingen?" asks the man.

"Harlingen, yes, please," Paloma says. "We"— she introduces us with a wave of her hand and holds up three fingers —"we tree."

The man opens the door. The car has light blue seats, very clean. The floor has little rugs. I have never been in such a car. We are wet enough to leave three big spots on the man's upholstery, I think. And we huddle together to be warm.

As we roll down the highway toward Harlingen, my mother heaves a sigh of relief and puts an arm around each of us. It is almost dark. One streak of bright yellow light shines in the west, under the black clouds. We are too tired to talk, even if the man speaks Spanish, which he doesn't seem to. The man reaches over and punches something on the dashboard. After a few minutes, it pops up. The man pulls it out, and it is red-hot on the end. He uses it to light another cigar.

Without a word, the man slows and turns, right there on the highway, and heads back toward Mexico.

"No!" Mama shouts.

Then, in a more controlled voice: "Please, *señor, no!*" She tries to open the door, though the car is still rolling. The door is locked. Paloma sits back and closes her eyes. She looks old suddenly, as if carved out of stone. Then she opens her eyes, reaches around, and squeezes us both to her.

"*Chicos,*" she says, "it appears we are going like the snail."

In almost no time at all, the big car comes to a quiet stop outside a military guardhouse. A flag of the United States flies above the roof, barely visible in the dusk. A soldier comes out and talks to the man driving the car. He opens the back door and leads us through the warm air into his little office. Ten minutes later, we are fetched by a Red Cross van and taken to jail.

15

Detention

THEY CALL THE JAIL a detention center. It's back down near the border but still in the U.S., in Texas. There are lots of people here. Thousands, I think, mostly from Guatemala and El Salvador. They have a name for us, not refugees anymore, but "illegal aliens." As if we had come sneakily from another planet.

They put us in a small room, bare except for two bunks, a cot, and a light bulb hanging down from the middle of the ceiling. At least we have walls around us, clean beds, food. I don't know about Mama and Romy, but I just don't feel like trying anymore. It's okay with me if somebody wants to take care of us.

WE WAKE UP to a buzzer. Our room is off a long, noisy corridor, full of crying babies, mothers talking, arguing, planning. There are no men. They're kept at the *corralón*, the "big corral," we're told. I picture them milling around in dust, surrounded by cowboys.

It seems to be morning, and a guard leads us to a cafeteria, full of steam and clanking pots. We get in a line, each pushing a tray, and some women give us plates of food, eggs and bread and some white stuff. I don't care that it has no salt. It feels good to eat.

A woman about Mama's age slaps her tray next to ours on the long table and sits down.

She's pale, with freckles, dark curly hair, earrings. She has small, bright, lively eyes. I feel right away that she is smart, and that she is sizing us up.

"You're new, aren't you?" she says.

Paloma nods. Romy and I watch the woman as we eat, and she watches Mama.

"Let me tell you a few things fast," she says. "My name's Carmen. I've been here awhile. I know something about this place, and I will help you if I can. Now listen. Are you listening?"

Paloma nods again.

"This is a detention center, and it is paid for by the U.S. government," says Carmen. "The people who run this place want to send you back where you came from. All three of you. *Fast*." Carmen sweeps her hand sideways across the table, getting rid of crumbs, or us. "They don't want to feed you. . . ." She gestures toward our trays. "They don't want to house you. . . ." She waves at the building around us. "And most of all, they don't want you moving into the United States." Carmen stabs a finger at us as she says this. Her fingernail is chewed down to the quick.

Paloma nods. She watches Carmen with narrowed eyes.

Carmen goes on. "This detention center is run according to laws, which are set out by the U.S. government. According to the laws of this country, you have a right to a hearing before they can send you back to wherever you've come from."

"El Salvador," says Paloma.

"Yes, me, too," says Carmen.

"What is a hearing?" Paloma asks.

"The laws of the United States say that you can come into the U.S. only if you can prove that you would have been killed if you had stayed at home. At your hearing they'll ask you a lot of questions in front of a judge, and the judge will decide whether you can stay."

"But, Mama, we don't *want*—" Romy was going to say that we don't want to stay in the U.S., that we only want to pass through on our way to Canada. Paloma must be kicking her foot under the table, however, because she stops right in the middle of the sentence.

Carmen looks at Romy a minute. Then she looks at me. "You following all this?"

I nod like Paloma, and swing my legs under the table and grab Romy's foot between mine.

"Mostly, they send everybody back," says Carmen.

Paloma swallows. She has stopped eating.

"It takes them three or four weeks to line up a hearing. So they'd rather not do it. They'd rather send you back today.

"That's where this form comes in." Carmen reaches into the back pocket of her jeans and pulls out a rumpled card, white with black writing printed on it.

She hands it to Mama.

"That is called a VDF, a Voluntary Deportation Form. If they can get you to sign that, they don't have to give you a hearing. If you sign that, you'll be on a plane to San Salvador tomorrow."

Carmen takes the card back. As she stands up to return her tray, she sticks it in her jeans pocket.

"I'll talk to you later," she says. "I'm on third east if you want to stop by. And, oh! One more thing." She pauses and looks at each of us. "There's no age limit on these Voluntary Deportation Forms. If *he* signs one"—she indicates me with her chin, since she is holding the tray with both hands—"if *he* signs one, they'll send him back without you."

We watch Carmen carry her tray to an opening in the wall, say something to someone in the kitchen, and then she is gone.

AFTER BREAKFAST, our hall guard takes us back to our room.

There isn't much to do. Romy and I play Rock, Fire, or Paper. Fire burns Paper. Paper covers Rock. Rock beats out Fire. When Romy wins, she punches my arm. When I win, I tickle her. When we both choose the same thing, we bump heads. It's boring, but better than nothing. Finally I have to roll over on my back to think. Romy wanders off down the hall to see if she can find other kids, while I stare at the light bulb over my head.

Everything Carmen told us is sinking into my mind.

I feel like old bubble gum—stretched thinner and thinner, farther and farther. Following Paloma, helping Paloma, obeying Paloma. Trying not to think of Jacinto, longing to be with Jacinto.

Carmen meant to warn us, I guess, but her words ring in my mind in a different way. "If you, Felipe, agree to it, they'll send you home."

And I hear Jacinto's warm, tired voice.

You are old enough, smart enough, tough enough.

Home. Jacinto. Rafa. Enrique. Abuela Ana. Chuy. For the first time in weeks, I let myself think of my dog, Payaso. Home. Payaso is leaping with joy.

All I have to do is sign my own name: Felipe Hernandez Ramirez. Nobody else has to sign. It's a decision I can make myself.

IN THE AFTERNOON, the guard brings a man to our room. Says he wants to talk to us. The man sits on the edge of my bunk, his clipboard on his knees. He wears jeans, but he also has a round collar like a priest.

He lets Mama ask him a lot of questions.

"Do you work for the authorities?"

"No, *señora*."

"For the government?"

"No, *señora*. I work for the church."

"Why are you here, then?"

"Because, *señora*"—he seems to be struggling for the right words—"because I have some, ah, friends, some contacts in San Salvador. In case you would like me to try to send a message, or make inquiries?"

News of Jacinto! We might be able to get news of Jacinto through this man! Paloma is cautious about giving Jacinto's name. So far, she's told the priest nothing about us.

"I would be careful not to release names to anyone other than my church contacts," the man says. "But it is of course entirely up to you."

"Yes!" says Mama. She claps her hands to her face. "No. Yes!"

We laugh, close to crying. Then she gives the priest our real names, address, Jacinto's workplace, everything. She gives him Rafa's name, as well. He asks our permission and begins writing it all down.

"The children's father is . . . deceased?" he asks quietly.

Mama takes a quick breath, looks at us and away.

Romy and I are very still, waiting for her answer.

"We don't know," she says at last.

The priest writes a little question mark on his paper, very neatly.

THE PRIEST in blue jeans leaves us, making no promises except that he will try to let Jacinto know where we are.

After he leaves, I don't want to play. I can't quite look my mother and sister in the eye. I need to be all alone to try and answer Jacinto's question. *Do you want everything that comes with knowing?*

Paloma drags Romy onto her bunk and begins braiding her hair in a fancy way.

I lie down on my cot and put my face close to the concrete wall. It has a cool smell like our walls at home.

BACK HOME we live on the slope of a volcano. Our side has not had a lava flow for a hundred years, though you know it's still alive because the ground rumbles deep down, and sometimes you can hear it or feel it. Grass and trees grow on our side of the mountain. Our part of town is outside and above a wall built by the government to keep lava and floods from destroying the city of San Salvador. Good for the city people, but not so good for us.

Once it rained very hard for two weeks. Mud came in a river from the mountain and backed up against the city wall. It slid against the wall right up through our town, thick yellow mud. When people or animals got stuck in it, they couldn't get out. The mud was heavy. It sucked things into itself and pushed over our neighbors' house as if it had been made of cards. In our house it just came in the downstairs part. We moved everything upstairs. After the water drew back, we scraped the mud off the walls. The mud sank into the concrete blocks and dried like clay, so it was hard to scrape. Mama did most of it while we were at school, but we helped in the evenings.

Jacinto calls our house the Casa Zorro. That's because on each of the side walls is a huge letter Z, which goes from the top of the house to the bottom. It was caused when the earth shook, just after the house was built. The walls cracked from top to bottom, but they didn't fall. Mama and Jacinto filled in the cracks with plaster, and the two Z's are whiter and brighter than the rest of the house.

We used to take picnics up to the crater of our volcano. From the top, the world is beautiful, the mountains green, the sea a mysterious blue in the distance. But looking across the crater always made me scared. Inside is mostly sliding sand and dirt. There are places, chimneys we call them, where wisps of steam and smoke rise up into the air. I used to think that they came from hell.

The possibility that Jacinto is dead, the possibility that he is alive and needs us, make a crater in the middle of our souls. The three of us, Paloma, Romy, and I, are camping on the edges, trying to make the best of it.

16

Day of the Dead

I WAKE UP. Where am I? Yes. The detention center. Why am I so jumpy?

I can go home! I can sign the form. I can find Jacinto. Whatever he is doing, I will help him do it.

And if he is dead?

If he is dead, I can find that out, too. We'll know, at least, that he doesn't need us.

THERE ARE WAKING-UP noises all up and down the hall.

"Where's Ana?" I hear Carmen call.

"Sent back."

"Where's María Luz?"

"Denied entry!"

And I hear Carmen say to her friend:

"There's only one way to prove eligible for U.S. entry."

"What's that?"

"Go back to El Salvador and let them shoot you."

Suddenly I'm not so sure.

CARMEN, I LEARN, was a university student in San Salvador. Her *compañero* was taken on the steps of the library, dragged kicking to a van, and shot. The authorities came for Carmen, but she got away. She doesn't mind talking about it in front of us. Carmen has been at the detention center for over a month, because she's pregnant. And she found a ruling saying that she can refuse deportation until her child is born.

Carmen is smart and she is angry. She uses her anger to make us all think. I thank her for it, and I hate her, too. Only yesterday I was happy to let Paloma tell me what to do. I was thinking, yes. Just to stay alive during the trip, we had to think all the time. But I wasn't questioning.

Even I am not always sure what is right to do. . . .

I listen to Jacinto's voice again and again in my mind. For the sound of it. For the comfort. It's the only conversation that seems real to me now.

Maybe that's what growing up really is. Not getting taller, but thinking for yourself. Questioning instead of just going along.

Growing up isn't something you necessarily want to do.

Here in the country, we don't even want our children to have birthdays anymore.

Growing up is something you decide to do. It takes courage.

I bet Carmen was talking in front of our door on purpose.

THE PEOPLE ACROSS the hall from us are country people. An older mother with three children, all younger than me. In the evening, when her children are asleep, Rosa Chavez tells Mama her story.

"My Chepe and our two big boys were working the corn. A truck came down the road. A little wind was blowing the other way, or we would have heard it. We would have hidden. I looked out from the yard, and there it was, pulled up close to the field.

"Soldiers got out, holding bags. I started running. . . ."

Rosa Chavez is crying. I close my eyes and lean against the wall, pretending to sleep.

Rosa stops crying and begins to talk softly with Mama. As they talk, I'm making plans. I remember hearing Carmen tell Rosa that she should expect to be sent back to El Salvador. Rosa has no proof of her burned-down house, no proof of her murdered husband and disappeared sons. Carmen says that, depending on what documentation the priest is able to get for us, there is a slim possibility of our being allowed to pass through the U.S. to Canada. But even if by some miracle Paloma and Romy and I get permission to enter the U.S., Rosa won't.

Knowing this, I gradually come to a decision. I will sign the form, and I'll travel home with the Chavez family.

The thing that will take the most courage is telling Mama, telling Romy.

I stop eating, and my stomach aches all the time.

I do what Paloma tells me, but it is as if I weren't here, as if I were watching from someplace else.

Even in our tiny room, I avoid Paloma. She works all day in the center's kitchen, and when she comes back, I lie on my cot, facing the wall, pretending to be asleep. Sometimes Mama sits down beside me and rubs my back. I don't talk to her.

A SCHOOL IS announced, to be held in the cafeteria. Paloma is all in favor. Romy and I are the first students there.

I hate the school. It's late October now, and there is talk of Halloween. This is what the Day of the Dead is called in the United States. Children go in to the streets in costume, my teacher says, and scare people and get candy.

I prefer the way we celebrate the Day of the Dead in El Salvador. Most families have many dead. Everyone who is left in the family gets together a picnic and some candles, and we go to the graveyard. We light the candles and play. The grown-ups tell stories that the people who are dead would have liked, or they sing songs. Then we have the picnic. That is what I would want to do for Jacinto, if he were dead. Eat chili peppers, which he loves. Play hopscotch on his grave.

Of course, a lot of the people who die don't get buried, back home. This is because maybe they are shot or disappeared, and their bodies are hidden or thrown into fields. The families can't find them. Then they don't know whether to celebrate the Day of the Dead or not.

In San Salvador, people from the Human Rights Office go around and take pictures of the bodies that are found every day. They keep the pictures in an office, so families can come and look at them if they want to find the body of their father or sister and bury it.

Thinking about it, I remember something from a long time ago. Once when Jacinto disappeared before, Mama went down to that office. She took me with her. She didn't let me see the pictures. I was very little then, and she just let me hold on to her leg. I could tell that she was nervous because she jiggled, and hummed a song with no tune under her breath. I remember women moaning softly, and once somebody cried very loud. It scared me so bad, I peed. When we left the office, there was a puddle where we had stood. I was worried about the puddle, but Mama didn't even notice. She hugged me a lot on the way home.

Our Day of the Dead is also called the Day of All the Saints. I don't guess that everybody who is dead is a saint. But I would think that all the people who have finished living have something good in them, just the way they did when they were alive.

Costumes and candy are okay with me. Still, it seems to me that Halloween separates us from dead people. If Jacinto were dead, would it make him scary? Would it make him into a monster?

I can't talk about this with Paloma because it would mean talking about Jacinto. I can't talk to Mama at all, because of what I need to tell her. Mama is busy trying to be practical. She spends her free time in Carmen's room, talking about laws and regulations.

I miss Abuela.

What would Abuela say if Jacinto were dead? Forget him, Felipe. You are lucky to be away from all that?

No!

Abuela would go with me to the cemetery. We would sit on a whitewashed concrete grave, sit in the sun until we felt warm, and we would talk. We would maybe split a beer and pour some on the ground for Jacinto. What shall we sing for Jacinto? Abuela would ask me. We would both think about it awhile. I would remember a song Jacinto liked, one Rafa sings.

I HUM THAT SONG to myself as I do my jobs around the center. Surely if Jacinto were dead, being dead would not make him bad. But I should go back to El Salvador to be near him. Even if it means that we might both be dead.

17

Family

I'VE JUST GOT TO TELL MAMA.
When I finally do tell her, it isn't because I'm
brave, but because I can't stand the suspense
any longer. Romy has gone across the hall to
play with the Chavez children, so Paloma and I
are in the room alone. Mama sewing something.
Me pretending to study.

"I want to go back, Mama."

It's out. I've imagined saying it so many times,
I'm not sure now that I've really spoken. Mama
is very still. Finally she looks up, her face small
and pinched. She doesn't waste time asking why.

"Jacinto told us to go to Canada."

"But he might need my help, Mama."

"If he had wanted you to stay, he would have told me, 'Leave Felipe with Rafa.' But no. He said, 'Take the children and go to Canada.' That is what Jacinto said." Her voice breaks, and tears well up in her eyes, but she keeps looking at me anyway, as if daring me to turn away.

"It's my place, Mama. El Salvador. I *want* to go back."

"They will make a soldier of you, Felipe. Or a courier for the *muchachos*. Either way you'll become a killer, and either way you will almost surely be killed. You are Salvadoran, yes. But you are not old enough or wise enough to help El Salvador yet."

She has practiced these words.

"But if Jacinto is there . . ."

"Jacinto wanted . . . wants you to live. Maybe he does hope you will go back to work in El Salvador when you are grown. And educated."

I let her words sink in. I don't want to argue. Mama isn't angry as I expected her to be, only sad. I see that, like me, she has been arguing with herself. And that Jacinto is in her mind, too.

"Mama," I say, "Jacinto and you and Romy and I, we're a family. We should do whatever we do together. And if we can't be all together, then

I think at least Jacinto shouldn't be all alone. You go to Canada with Romy if you can find a way. I'll go find Jacinto."

"Felipe," she replies, "we *are* a family. And Jacinto has asked us to go to Canada so that he can find us there, so that you and Romy can grow up away from war.

"But if you sign that form, which I pray every day you will not, then I'll sign it, too, and so will Romy. Because we stay together."

Then, for the first time since we got the note under our door, tears start running down my face. Once they start, there's no stopping. For everybody I miss, for the sadness people have at home, for the decisions we all have to make.

The more I think about it, the more tears come. The only place to be alone in the center is a stall in the bathroom, and I stay in there until many people have banged on the door in impatience. After forever, I sneak out and wrap myself up in a sheet and lie on my cot, leaning my hot, wet face against the concrete wall, feeling light and empty and sad as a gourd.

TWO DAYS LATER, I'm in the storage closet, shelving supplies for the janitor. The priest in blue jeans comes to see me. "Felipe," he says. "There you are."

Por supuesto.

"We have received a letter from your friend Rafael. Addressed to your mother, who has let me read it."

I look at him and away. He's a kind man, and he looks uncomfortable.

"Not from Jacinto?" I manage to ask.

"Rafael has written that your father, Jacinto, is dead, Felipe. Rafael held a funeral for him, and many friends were there. Rafael is very sad and sends his sympathy and affection."

The priest looks down at the backs of his hands.

I feel nothing at all. Empty.

The priest asks if I would like to see the letter from Rafa.

"Yes."

Anything that has anything to do with Jacinto is better than nothing.

The priest unfolds the letter for me, hands it to me. I read it over slowly. I find out things that the priest didn't tell me—that Jacinto's body, or a body they think was Jacinto's, was left in front of his workplace. The man they think was

Jacinto had been shot many times in the head. They could not be sure it was Jacinto, but Rafael knew him by his build and by his shoes.

SOMEONE COULD HAVE stolen his shoes. Other men are his size.

I GET A SUDDEN feeling that Jacinto is there in the supply closet, his arm over my shoulder.

Then it goes away, and I am alone, disbelieving and angry.

I stay in the supply closet, numbly breaking open boxes and stacking rolls of toilet paper. When I finally get enough courage to go back up to our room, Romy is asleep on her bunk, with tears on her face, and Mama is sitting on the floor playing cards with Carmen. She doesn't look different. For a second, I make myself think she doesn't care. And I hate her.

Jacinto. Say something about Jacinto.

She sees me, slaps down her cards and opens her arms. I run to her and she hugs me, and then, before I cry, she starts pummeling me. My fighting instincts take over, and we roll on the floor, wrestling. Paloma sits up, wipes tears off her face with her sleeve, and calls out to Carmen:

"Come finish the game!"

At night the doctor gives Mama two blue sleeping pills. He asks if I want one.

"No."

The only way I'll see Jacinto now is if I dream about him.

18

Rock, Fire, Paper

AS I SAID, there is always a lot of commotion on our corridor. The loudest thing of all is the loudspeaker. It hangs in the corner of the ceiling, a big, gray metal megaphone. Every once in a while, it growls as if about to explode. Then a gravelly voice makes an announcement, first in English, then in Spanish. The English gives all the mothers a chance to quiet their children. By the time the Spanish comes on, everyone is silent and listening hard, mothers nursing their babies to keep them quiet.

As soon as the loudspeaker crackles and is silent, everyone starts questioning one another.

"What did he say?"

"What did that mean?"

"Representatives of Project Canada are now available at the legal building to interview persons interested in applying for Canadian citizenship. If you are interested in applying for Canadian citizenship, please notify your warden immediately."

Mama is sitting on the floor, rearranging scraps of cloth. She puts down her needle and slaps her hands on her knees.

"Chicos!"

We are studying for school, copying verbs in English and muttering them aloud.

> I go
> You go
> He/she/it goes

"We go!" yells Paloma triumphantly. "Warden! Warden, please! *We* go to Canada!"

"Okay, okay," says the warden, walking slowly down the hall, smacking gum. "Don't get excited."

Paloma grabs the hairbrush and neatens us up. Carmen comes running down the hall. She kisses Paloma on both cheeks.

"This is your one chance," I hear her say in Mama's ear. "Knock their socks off."

THE WARDEN LEADS us out into the exercise yard, where a little house has been set up. The kind you bring in on a truck, and that people sell ice cream from back home. There is a long line already. On the door of the house is a flag, red and white with a red maple leaf.

"That's the flag of Canada," Paloma tells Romy.

TWO HOURS in the sun, and then we are inside. Two men and a woman sit behind a table covered with papers. We sit across from them. One of the men is a translator.

They ask our names, our ages, how we like the volunteer school, how we like our jobs at the detention center. And finally they ask us questions about home. These are the questions we expect, the questions Paloma spent hours preparing answers to, with Carmen. What surprises me is that the two interviewers and the interpreter listen. They ask questions not to trap us but to find out more. They write things down, careful to get them right.

Mama leans forward as she talks to them. She looks straight at them, gesturing with her hands. Even where she was advised not to, she speaks the truth, only changing people's names.

PALOMA HAS ANSWERED many questions. The interviewers look at each other, and there is a silence.

One of the men clears his throat and carefully asks, through the interpreter:

"Do you understand that you have broken the law by entering the United States without permission?"

"Yes," says my mother firmly.

"And yet you intend to be a law-abiding citizen of Canada?"

"Yes," Paloma says.

Doubt hangs in the air. To everyone's surprise, Romy leans forward suddenly and puts her hands on the desk.

"It's like a game we play," she says. "Rock, Fire, or Paper." She clears her throat. "One of them is always stronger." She looks across the table at the interviewers, holding her breath while the translator speaks.

"You have two things of big importance, see." She balls her hands into fists. The interpreter translates. Everyone in the room is staring at Romy. It's very quiet. Then Romy stalls. Her mouth opens, but no words come out.

"She means," I say, "that you have the law." Romy taps her left fist on the gray metal table. The interpreter says just one word.

"And you have life." Romy brings down her right fist. The interpreter says one more word. It seems too short.

"She means . . . ," I say, hoping I'm right, "she means that life is stronger." The interviewers speak together softly. One laughs, pulls out a bandanna, blows his nose.

Romy covers her left fist with her right hand and nods.

THE INTERVIEWERS recommend us for Canadian citizenship. A group of North Americans helps us out with the jail fines. Regular people, not authorities. They agree to help us find a place to stay in the United States until our Canadian papers are ready.

Because of Romy.

"Because of both of you," says Mama, hugging us together.

"All of us," I remind her. "And Carmen."

"And especially Carmen," Paloma says.

"And Jacinto," says Carmen.

Good old Carmen. With Jacinto's name, she breaks a spell, makes us as complete as we can be. And Paloma is crying at last.

19

North

A FEW MORE DAYS at the detention center. More people are arriving, and another family shares our room. At night the floor is covered with people trying to sleep. The priest in blue jeans has contacts in the North as well as in El Salvador. He's trying to find a place for us to live.

"In Canada?" asks Romy.

"It will be at least six months before you are allowed to move to Canada," he tells us.

"So where will we live until then? Will we stay here?" Romy looks worried. She is getting taller, thin now, all eyes. At the detention center,

Romy tells me, there isn't enough air. She has headaches and bad dreams.

"No," the priest answers. "I'm looking for a family in the northern United States, close to Canada. In the state of Wisconsin. A family who will have a room for you, who will want you to come stay with them. There you can learn English and get used to the cold weather. And then, when your papers are completed, you can move to Canada."

"Will we have to go to school?" asks Romy.

"Yes," say Mama and the priest at the same time.

"Could we stay on our own in Wisconsin?" Paloma asks. "Do we have to stay in someone else's house?"

"It will be better for you to stay at someone's house," the priest answers.

Later, I ask Mama why it will be better. Like her, I long for us to be our own again.

Paloma answers carefully, "I'm not sure that the priest can know what is better for us. But I do know that he is doing all he can to help. This is the time to say thank you and be nice."

I must have made a face, because she raises her eyebrows at me in a warning way. "The priest and his friends will help us get to Canada. That's what is important. If you want to argue, argue with me." She twists my arm behind my back in a sudden move Jacinto used to make when he wanted to start a wrestling match.

THIS IS OUR LAST WEEK here, and we get inspected a lot. A doctor comes and shines a flashlight in our ears and up our noses.

"Well," asks Mama, "do these look like Canadian noses?"

The doctor laughs way down in his stomach. He speaks Spanish.

"They'll do for Canadian noses" is the verdict.

THE DAY BEFORE we are to leave, Rosa Chavez and her family are sent back to El Salvador. Hugs and kisses. Romy gives the youngest Chavez her Cipitio, for luck. Crying and blessings, and then a big silence inside. I ask permission to help Paloma wash pots in the kitchen. Soapy water, shining aluminum, clanging and banging.

THE PRIEST in blue jeans drives us north on the first day. We've finally learned to call him *Padre* Jim.

WE STAY in many homes on the way to Wisconsin, each for a day or two. Strangers make their houses warm for us and cook us good meals. At each place people give us clothes, boots, sweaters. Romy and I are nice. We say thank you many times. We try hard to answer questions in English. We discover jigsaw puzzles, which allow you to lie on the floor quietly playing, listening to the grown-ups—piecing together the conversations, the attitudes of our hosts. It seems that although the U.S. government does bad things in El Salvador and supplies the weapons with which we are killed, many North Americans have good hearts. Confused and regretful, they discuss ways of changing the policies of their leaders. They ask Paloma to make speeches to church groups, to newspapers. Paloma refuses. I hear her tell a church minister:

"My own anger and confusion are too great. I want to lead an ordinary life."

OUR LAST DRIVER has so many boxes in the front seat that he lets us all sit together in back. We snuggle up under a blanket he has back there, which is covered with dog hairs. I'm glad. You get tired of trying to talk to foreigners and smiling all the time.

Snow is a big surprise. We are in mountains somewhere, and the night sky is black. Shreds of white blow in the headlights and stick to the side window. They seem to be alive, to be trying to tell us something. The road is white and slippery, and we go very slowly. In front of us climbing the mountain is a huge truck carrying trunks of trees. One will surely slide out, right down onto our car.

"*Mamí* . . . ," says Romelia, too scared to talk.

"*Chicos,*" says Mama matter-of-factly, "we haven't come all this way to die in Wisconsin."

Then she curls up and goes to sleep.

20

Wisconsin

SHE'S RIGHT; WE DON'T DIE. By dawn we are driving through farmland covered with white snow, gentle land that rolls in waves like the sea. We drive up to the Andersons' house, standing tall and alone along the side of the road.

The Andersons are kind, quiet, religious people, as old as Chuy and Abuela, although some of their children are teenagers. At first they are too careful of us. As if, as Paloma says, we were little birdies just fallen from the nest.

MORE THAN A HUNDRED DAYS go by. Days of school and sledding on dazzling snow. Painful English lessons. Shots, hearing tests. Nights of howling blizzards, snuggled safe in the Andersons' big wooden farmhouse under quilts thick with goose feathers. And waiting, always waiting for papers to make us legal, so that we can go to Canada. I wonder, sometimes, why we even want to go to Canada now.

"We have to live somewhere, Felipe," says Romy. She's right, of course. I just wish it could be at home.

PALOMA HAS TAKEN up motor mechanics. Mr. Anderson lets her tinker with the tractor. She is not as careful as Jacinto was, and she gets oil all over. Mr. Anderson says she is a natural grease monkey. Paloma keeps her hair short and dresses in the clothes people bring me: corduroys and flannel shirts, a down vest. Sometimes people mistake her for my shorter brother.

For now, without Jacinto, I think Paloma has no use for being a woman. For now, I'm glad.

SPRING. Squiggly lines of geese fly over, and ducks, too. Honking, barking like dogs, happy to be going north, while we still wait. Little duck, Abuela called me. I wish I were

162 ■

a duck. Or a goose. An invincible Salvadoran-Canadian gander. Able to span continents with my strong wings.

PALOMA AND MRS. ANDERSON are making tortillas. The Andersons' daughter Mary is grating cabbage and cutting up carrots. I'm on the kitchen floor with Barkus, the dog.

The sun is shining and a sprinkling of green appears all over the fields, so light it seems like a trick of the eyes. April.

Romy is talking on the phone to a friend from school. She talks in English, saying things she has heard the Anderson children say on the phone.

"Hi!"

"What's up?"

There are many long pauses. Giggles. The rest of us laugh at her, and Romy makes faces at us. Paloma is of two minds about our having American friends. She wants us to be happy about going to Canada.

Mr. Anderson comes in with a slip of yellow paper.

"Registered mail—*Very Important*—for Mrs. Hernandez Ramirez," he announces, presenting the slip to Paloma. "Must be picked up at the post office in the next five minutes."

Paloma and Mrs. Anderson run for the car. Romy and I hop in the back. Mrs. Anderson has trouble getting the car started. Paloma has trouble not yelling. We run a yellow light and pull up in front of the post office. Forget the meter. Romy and I take the steps three at a time. Inside, the P.O. window is very high. Mama, Romy, and I line up, our chins just above the counter. With a huge grin, Paloma hands the postman the yellow slip. He stands up there like Santa Claus, like God. A kind look on his face. Paloma has her hands joined as if in prayer. Her face shines with anticipation.

"*You* are Mrs. Ramirez?"

"Yes!"

An official envelope is handed down, ripped open. Visas spill out, instructions, official seals. The postman leans over in curiosity. Paloma grabs his neck and plants a kiss on his cheek. Everyone in the P.O. seems amazed. Most especially Paloma and the postman.

We go back to the Andersons' house, our house.

We put Romy on the phone: spread the word, invite friends.

Make more tortillas.

Celebrate.

"Imagine . . . ," says Paloma, our papers spread before her like treasure. Friends and neighbors come over, carrying platters of potato salad, chicken, beans. Tears fill Paloma's eyes. She quickly jumps up and starts setting the table.

"*Chicos!*" she says. "Can't you see that we need more chairs?"

"*Siempre a sus órdenes,*" I tell her. I bow to her with my hand over my heart. "Always at your service."

She laughs, and I see gold flecks in her eyes. She knows how I mean it and don't mean it.

Don't miss

FRANCES TEMPLE'S

Taste of Salt

A STORY OF MODERN HAITI

Winner of the 1993
Jane Addams Children's Book Award

"Gripping. . . . The combination of dramatic action, romantic interest, and vivid storytelling will grab even the most apolitical teens." (boxed review)   —ALA *Booklist*

"Lyrical . . . no background knowledge is needed to become caught up in the drama of the many in this embattled land as related through the eyes of two compelling characters. An excellent first effort." (starred review)
—*School Library Journal*

"Arresting . . . a powerful fictional portrait of the poverty and oppression in contemporary Haiti." (starred review)
—*Publishers Weekly*

"Temple handles, with unobtrusive ease, the intricacies of changing and emerging viewpoints, the juxtaposition of past and present, the blend of political and personal, the balance of romance and violence." (starred review)
—*Bulletin of the Center for Children's Books*

"A deeply felt, provocative statement of human courage by an exciting new author." (starred review)
—*The Horn Book*